The Clue of

the Four Wigs

by G. H. Teed

A London Detective Drama.
By the Author of the popular
"Dr. Huxton Rymer" Series.
Originally published in
The Sexton Blake Library by Amalgamated Press,
dated 1925, No. 16 (New Series).

Stillwoods Edition 2018

Quote:
Four New Volumes of the <u>Sexton Blake Library</u> are issued on the first Friday of every month. Please give your Newsagent a Standing Order for the Leading Detective-Story Magazine." (1925)

Catalogue Information:
Title: The Clue of the Four Wigs
Author: G. H. Teed (George Heber Hamiton Teed (1886-1938))
First Published: The Sexton Blake Library, No. 16 in the New Series, 1925.
This Publication: Stillwoods, 2018.
Blog: Stillwoods.Blogspot.Ca
Storefront: http://www.lulu.com/spotlight/lulubook22
ISBN Canada: 978-1-988304-52-6

The cover of this Stillwoods Edition is adapted from the original Sexton Blake Library serial publication.

1. The Quiet Suburban Villa—Tragedy and Mystery.

MR. JOHN MCMINN blotted, folded and thrust into its envelope the letter he had been writing. He inscribed the address with the meticulous care of one who is not a prolific letter writer and who has an ingrained suspicion that no communication will reach its proper destination, unless each letter is formed in such a way that no possible doubt can exist as to its meaning.

He dried the fresh ink methodically, after which he placed a stamp neatly and correctly in the upper right-hand corner. Then he rose.

"I shall be back in a few moments, my dear," he announced, addressing his wife, a buxom blonde who sat in an expansive easy-chair near the window, through which she could command a view of a considerable portion of the road which ran past the tiny garden in front of the house.

The woman who had been drowsing, as corpulent people will after a full and satisfying meal, nodded mechanically at the sound of his voice, and John McMinn passed out into the hall.

It was a warm evening in mid-summer, so he donned only a light soft hat on his way to the front door. He opened this, leaving it slightly ajar against his return; then he walked down the diagonal path to the front gate.

Dusk was just gathering into full night. In the tree-lined road in which the villa was situated, the shadows were already pools of gloom where the branches hung low, and John McMinn half smiled to himself as he saw a couple here and a couple there, standing close together as young folks a-courting are wont to stand when friendly night enfolds them.

He was a friendly soul, was John McMinn, and no residents of Woodberry Down were more respected in the whole Finsbury Park district than he and his wife.

They were a childless couple, but it was common knowledge among neighbours and friends who had known them during the fifteen years they had lived there, that the only regret in their lives was that no child had come to them. They were quiet-living folk—highly respectable, regular attendants at church, hospitable when opportunity offered and, it was said, comfortably happy.

Mr. McMinn was chief foreman of the printing-room of one of the largest London dailies. He was popular both with his employers and the men under him.

He was a conscientious member of two local lodges, a member of the local council, and not so radical in his political views that the more conservative element of the district need feel any nervousness about including him in any local affair.

His wife, the large, placid-looking blonde, whom he had left sitting by the window in the sitting-room of the semi-detached villa which they occupied, was quite as well thought of as her husband.

She was extremely charitable (it was generally understood that she had quite considerable private means of her own), was a regular attendant at the weekly Thursday afternoon reading circle, always ready with a subscription to any local affair, or equally willing to give her services, if required, and, while a little "heavy" at times, was regarded as a highly desirable fixture in the district.

The villa itself was typical of its class. Semi-detached, it joined that which was occupied by a well-to-do wholesale fishmonger. It was not large, consisting of four rooms on the ground floor and four rooms above, with two unfurnished rooms forming an attic.

On the ground floor there was the sitting-room, a large apartment somewhat over-furnished, the sideboard being a little too massive, the table a little too long, the chairs a trifle too ornate, and the pictures confined entirely to subjects which included fish, game and fruits.

Across the hall was a parlour, which was jammed with a heterogeneous collection of stuff, which was in shocking bad taste, but which filled the soul of John McMinn with unctuous joy.

Back of that was a small breakfast-room and conservatory combined, and from this tiny room, which was seldom used, a short flight of steps led from a so-called French window into a narrow strip of garden, which ran down to the bank of the New River just before that lazy stream empties into the great reservoir which is one of London's water reserves.

One servant sufficed for the simple needs of the house, and, as usual, on this Sunday evening she was out. It was the custom of the McMinn's to have their Sunday dinner in the middle of the day, and a cold supper after returning from church in the evening. Thus it was possible for the servant to have most of the day to herself.

This particular day had been the same as any other Sunday. They had supped half an hour or so before John McMinn began his letter. Ordinarily he would not have been there at that hour at all, for, as foreman of the printing-room of the great daily paper where he worked, his duties began at six o'clock in the evening, and carried him on until four o'clock the following morning.

Though it was not until after six o'clock that he arrived home, for he invariably took a light breakfast in the vicinity of Broad Street Station, before catching one of the early underground trains to Finsbury Park.

But he had not been at his work since the previous Thursday, owing to a sprained wrist. Thus the ordinary arrangements of the household had been somewhat altered, except for this day, the Sunday, when he usually managed to be at home.

Most of his leisure hours were spent in the little garden at the back, and the letter he was about to post was nothing more important than a request for a new book on gardening which he had seen advertised in one of the Sunday papers.

He closed the wooden gate behind him, and walked leisurely up the road towards the pillar-box, some forty or fifty yards away. As he went along he passed one or two neighbours, to whom he nodded a cheerful good-evening; then, on reaching the box, he slipped his letter in and started back towards his home.

He stood at the gate for perhaps half a minute, drinking in the warm summer night; then he turned and passed up the path to the open door. He closed it after him, and, since he did not intend going out again, locked it before hanging up his hat.

He pushed open the sitting-room door and paused just inside, his hand on the switch of the electric light.

"Shall I turn on the light, my dear?" he asked, looking towards the heap in the easy-chair.

There was no answer, and John McMinn smiled in the dusk.

"Sound asleep," he murmured indulgently. "But if she goes on any longer now, she will be awake half the night. It is always the case. So I'll wake her. And, anyway," he added, as if it were an afterthought, "I want to read."

With that he pressed the switch and crossed the room towards the window. He passed the chair and drew the curtain. Then, with a half-smile, he turned and laid one hand on his wife's shoulder.

"Come on, my dear," he said, shaking her gently. "Must wake up now—you won't sleep later if you nap too long now."

But again there was no answer, and, for the first time since entering the room, John McMinn looked fully at his wife. Her eyes were closed, and she was lying back as if in a sound sleep. He shook her again, this time more forcibly, and was about to call to her more loudly when, suddenly, her body lolled forward, and before he could catch hold of her, had rolled off the chair on to the floor.

John McMinn was frightened, and looked it. He stared down at her for a few moments, his eyes wide with wonder; then he dropped to his knees and began shaking her vigorously. But there was no response.

She had fallen half on her side, with her face turned away from him, and now, with some difficulty, he managed to get her over on her back. It was then that a strange chill crept into the heart of John McMinn He bent over her closely and touched her face.

It was quite warm, and it would have been hard for him to believe that she was not just asleep, but for an indefinable something about the complete relaxation of the body.

He drew back and made to lay his hand on her heart. She was wearing a black silk blouse, and it was not until his hand touched it that he discovered it was wet and sticky in the front.

Again that chill entered into his heart as he jerked his hand away. It felt warm, moist, horrible. He held it up and looked at it. Then a startled gasp of horror broke from him as he saw that the palm and the outer side were stained a dull crimson.

Another gasp escaped him, and then he began to shake from head to foot as if the palsy had gripped him. It was the first time in his life that John McMinn had ever seen anything like that. The shock was so terrific that, for an appreciable space of time his wits refused to function.

Then the heavy wave of fright passed, and once more he drove himself to touch the front of his wife's dress.

His fingers caressed the soft satin timorously. He forced himself to lift the tip of one finger and look at it.

"Blood!"

The word escaped in a terror-laden whisper, and his eyes half-closed as he thought he was fainting. He fought for self-control, and succeeded in conquering the acute nausea which was sweeping over him in waves.

He bent down, his startled gaze fixed on that dark, wet patch on the black satin. Now he could see a hole in the fabric, and into his brain beat the ominous words:

"She is dead! She is dead! She is dead!"

He rocked back on his heels and stumbled to his feet. He stood gazing helplessly about the room, trying to think what he should do. He made as if to call the servant, but then he remembered she would not be back until eleven. Something told him to get the doctor, and he staggered to the telephone in the hall.

With shaking fingers he took down the book and fumbled about until he found the page on which was the name of a local practitioner. He managed to speak the number to the operator, and a few moments later heard a voice at the other end of the wire.

He managed to give his name, and ask the doctor to come quickly. He heard that gentleman assure him that he would be there inside ten minutes. Then John McMinn hung up the receiver and staggered back into the sitting-room.

But just inside the door he paused. He tried to advance, but could not bring himself to do so. He backed out into the hall again and lurched along to the front door. He opened this, forgetting that his hand had stained the wall and was marking the handle of the door.

He reached the porch, and there he stood until a small two-seater car drew up outside the gate. A young man entered briskly, slamming the gate so hard that John McMinn jumped as if a pistol had been fired.

The young man did not see him until he had almost reached the porch. Then he halted abruptly:

"You are Mr. McMinn? You telephoned for Dr. Graydon? He is away, and I am acting as his locum. What is the trouble, Mr. McMinn?"

McMinn made a gesture, bidding him enter. He led the way along the hall, and pushed open the door of the sitting-room. He then pointed towards the prone woman on the floor.

"There, doctor," he gasped, "there—my wife—see to her."

The young locum hastened across and dropped to his knees beside the woman. He bent over her and started to lay a hand over her heart. As his flesh came into contact with the sticky stain he uttered an exclamation of distaste and drew his hand away.

He looked at it, and then his brow lowered. One glance was sufficient for him. He shot a look at McMinn and then he went to work, swiftly, efficiently, and with a care that would have done credit to a much older man.

John McMinn watched him, fascinated, afraid and shaking. The young locum paid him no attention until he had been at work for several minutes. Then, suddenly he sat up and turned his keen eyes on the other.

"When did this happen? And how?" he asked curtly.

"I—I don't know," answered McMinn hoarsely. "Is she—is she—dead, doctor?"

"Yes. Your wife is dead, Mr. McMinn. She has been killed by some missile entering her heart—a bullet, I should think. What do you know about it?"

"I—I—nothing, doctor. I found her like that—in the chair—thought she was asleep —shook her—rolled her on the floor—found that stain on her dress and telephoned for you. Oh, my Heaven! Dead! It can't be!"

The doctor rose.

"I shall do what I can," he said curtly. "But this is a matter for the police! Where is your telephone?"

2. How Sexton Blake Became Acquainted With the Case—No Ordinary Crime.

MR. SEXTON BLAKE, accompanied by his young assistant, Tinker, was on his way across the stone-paved courtyard at New Scotland Yard when he saw his friend, Detective-inspector Thomas, coming in through the big main arch.

The inspector paused for a moment beneath the electric-light there to speak to the constable on duty, and he was just on the point of proceeding, when Blake and Tinker came up. As the inspector saw them he pulled up sharply.

"Hallo, Blake—hallo, young 'un. Where are you off to, Blake?"

"We are on our way home," answered Blake, shaking hands. "I have just been up to see Coutts on a little business. How are things?"

"Not so bad—been a little slack lately. I'm just off to investigate a case out at Finsbury Park—looks like murder from what I can gather. Would you care to come? I can't promise anything, but it might possess some interesting points."

"Murder, eh! When did it happen?"

"This evening, apparently. The report was telephoned through to the yard and was passed on to me in Piccadilly. I am just going to get the car and go along. If you haven't anything better to do, join me."

"All right, we'll come. We have nothing in particular to do, and it will be a blow at any rate."

They turned and accompanied the inspector along to the garage beyond the colonnade. The big grey police car was always ready for instant use, and in a few moments the police chauffeur had backed it out into the court.

Tinker got in the front seat while Blake and the inspector entered the tonneau; then it thundered, off along the Embankment on its way to Aldwych and Roseberry Avenue.

The inspector could tell Blake very little more than he had already communicated. The report, he said, had been 'phoned in from Finsbury Park by the local inspector.

A woman had been found dead in a villa in Woodberry Down, a road near the Manor House Corner, and both the doctor, who had been called in first, as well as the divisional police surgeon, thought it looked like murder. That was all.

So they discussed other matters until the big car raced along the Seven Sisters Road, up past the park and across the Manor House

Corner into the road known as Woodberry Down.

It drew up at a house situated well along the road and Blake concluded that, so far, the neighbourhood was unaware of what had happened for there was no curious crowd hanging about in front.

They got out as soon as the car stopped, and, following the inspector through the gate and up the path, paused on the porch.

The inspector did not press the bell, but, rapped on one of the glass panels with his knuckles. The door was opened almost at once by a constable who saluted and drew back.

They passed into a narrow hall lighted by a single electric bulb, and following a gesture of the constable's, walked along to a door on the right. The door of this room was partly ajar and, as the inspector pushed it open, Blake could hear low voices inside.

He entered with Tinker close at his heels and saw that there were four men present, one of whom, it was obvious, had no connection with the police. This individual, a small, nondescript man of early middle age was seated on a stiff chair in one corner, his head resting in his hands.

The other three were standing by the centre table, two of them talking while the other listened closely to what was being said. This latter individual, Blake saw, was a police inspector, while it did not take him long to fix the other two as doctors.

All three turned as they entered, and the inspector saluted Inspector Thomas. He then indicated the other two, introducing one as Dr. Pearson, the divisional police surgeon, and the other as Dr. Graydon.

Then Blake and Tinker were introduced and at the mention of the famous criminologist's name the two physicians gazed at him keenly.

And now for the first time the newcomers saw the body of a stout woman lying on the floor close to a big chair near the window. Inspector Thomas strode forward while the junior inspector moved close and began rapidly giving him particulars of the case in the short, clipped police manner.

"It looks like murder," he said. "The husband is there in the corner—name is John McMinn, foreman printer on the London Daily X, can't give us any information as to how it happened. His story is that he and his wife were sitting in this room after supper. She was in this chair, dozing, while he was writing a letter. It was just a little before ten and dusk when he went out to post the letter. Everything was perfectly normal when he left. The pillar-box is only a matter of forty or fifty yards up the road. He walked straight there, posted his letter and walked straight back.

"When he entered the room he asked his wife if they should have the light on. He got no answer and thought she was sleeping. He switched on the light and then closed the blind. It was when he had done that he turned to wake her. She did not answer him so he shook her by the shoulder. She rolled out of the chair on to the floor. He thought she had fainted, so knelt down. He put his hand on her heart and found the front of her dress wet. Looked at his hand and saw blood.

"When be recovered from the shock he went to the telephone and called Dr. Fraser's house. Dr. Fraser is away, but Dr. Graydon is acting as his locum, and it was he who came. On his arrival he found McMinn on the front porch waiting for him. They came in here, and a few moments after he began his examination Dr. Graydon saw that the woman was dead. He drew away the dress and found a wound just over the heart.

"He did not proceed further then, but called the nearest police station. Dr. Pearson was notified and came on at once. I met him here. He has made an examination of the body and agrees with Dr. Graydon that death was due to some missile entering the heart—probably a bullet. I 'phoned the Yard and since then we have just been waiting for your arrival. Beyond what was necessary for the examination the body has not been moved."

He paused then, and with a nod Inspector Thomas knelt down. Blake and Tinker moved closer and watched while the inspector made a brief examination. When he rose he turned to the divisional doctor.

"Will you show me your notes, please?" he asked.

The doctor handed him a pad and Blake leant over his shoulder while he studied it. At one point Inspector Thomas paused and looked over his shoulder at Blake.

"See that?" he asked. "Have a go at it, Blake."

Blake dropped to his knees, and placing one hand on the head of the dead woman gently moved it until he brought away a thick blonde wig, revealing that she had been almost bald. He showed it to the inspector, then he replaced it carefully.

"A good piece of work," he commented as he rose. "I shouldn't have guessed it at a casual glance."

"Nor I," returned the other.

They proceeded to read the rest of the notes, after which Inspector Thomas turned to John McMinn.

"You have told all you know?" he asked.

McMinn nodded.

"Every word," he answered in muffled, broken tones.

"Have you any suspicions of anyone?"

"None."

"You know of no enemies who would do this?"

"No—my wife—I—we hadn't an enemy in the world."

"And you say it happened in the time it took you to walk to the pillar-box and back?"

"Yes—not more than seven or eight minutes."

"You heard or saw no one?"

"No one—nothing."

Suddenly the inspector turned to the local man.

"Come into another room," he said. "We can talk there."

All hands passed into the hall where the local inspector signed for the constable to keep an eye on the sitting-room. He then opened another door on the right and they entered the dining-room where they could see the remains of a meal on the table.

At that moment there came a sound, seemingly at the back of the house, and the six were standing in a group just inside the door when a young woman entered. She was wearing a hat and coat as if she had just returned to the house and, at sight of the strangers, she gave a startled gasp.

"Who are you?" asked the inspector sharply.

"The maid, sir," she stammered.

"Your night out, I suppose?"

"Yes, sir."

"Only just returned?"

"Yes, sir."

"Where have you been?"

"To—to Hampstead, sir."

"Very well. Go to the kitchen and remain there. I may want to speak with you later."

Wide-eyed and frightened, the girl retired and closed the door. Then Inspector Thomas turned to the local man. He made a gesture with his thumb towards the sitting-room.

"Did he do the job?" he asked.

The local man shook his head.

"I can't say. We found no weapon of any sort and he seems to talk straight enough."

"They all do that," grunted Inspector Thomas. "She didn't shoot herself if there is no weapon. And if she didn't, then it is murder. Let me have what you know about these people."

With that he leant against the table and drew out a cigar. As for Sexton Blake he drew closer, for he had conceived a very sudden interest in what was already promising to be no ordinary case.

3.   Seeking Clues—The "Yard" Man's Line of Reasoning—Sexton Blake's Interest in the Victim's Wig.

INSPECTOR BROWN, the local man, coughed diffidently. Detective-inspector Thomas was one of the "Big Five" at the Yard, and it was but natural that the lesser official should be swept by nervousness in his presence.

Moreover, there was the famous detective, Sexton Blake, present as well, and never before had Brown been confronted with quite such an affair as this.

He managed to collect himself, however, and in response to Thomas' request said:

"I know these people, the McMinn's, quite well. They have been living in the district for fifteen years or so. They have always borne the very highest sort of reputation. McMinn is, as I said, foreman of the printing shop of the London Daily X—. He is a member of some local lodges and is on the local council. They are quiet living folk—or were—and are regular attendants of the church to which I belong. In fact, chief, they have both been at my house several times. Mrs. McMinn and my wife have served on several church committees together and my wife has always spoken most highly of both of them."

"Um. I take it, then, you don't think McMinn did the job."

"Well, chief, it would be difficult for me to do so."

Inspector Thomas glanced towards Blake. "There's a nut for you to crack, Blake," he said. "Murder—cold murder—no weapon found yet—quiet living folk, living a humdrum suburban existence—not a thing known against either of them over fifteen years— what do you make of it?"

Blake removed his cigarette.

"I should prefer not to give an opinion— yet," he answered. "We have only seen the body. An examination of the premises may reveal something. If McMinn was out, as he says, when the murder took place, then we have to look for someone else. The murderer was either concealed in the house before McMinn went to post his letter or he entered it during his brief absence."

"The first thing we did was to search every room in the house and the grounds," broke in the local inspector. "We didn't find a thing."

"I haven't been in the house very long, but I discovered something on entering," remarked Blake contemplatively. "I didn't pay much attention to it at the time, but now—I don't know. I think we might make a closer examination."

"What was it?" asked Thomas in a puzzled way.

"The handle of the front door is of some white composition. I was the last to enter with the exception of Tinker. As I closed the door I noticed a dark stain on the handle and as I turned round several other streaky stains on the wall. Are they blood? If so, how did they get there? It may be that McMinn left them there when he went to the porch to wait for the doctor; or—it may have been left there by the murderer."

Inspector Thomas flung round towards the local man.

"Did you see that?" he asked sharply.

"N—no, I didn't," acknowledged Brown rather sheepishly. "I didn't examine the walls."

Inspector Thomas snorted and motioned for Dr. Pearson to come with him. They left the dining-room together, followed by Brown and the young locum. Blake and Tinker were left alone and, as the others disappeared, Tinker looked at Blake and solemnly winked. But Blake disregarded the lad. He stood leaning against the table studying the end of his cigarette until Inspector Thomas returned.

"By thunder, Blake, but I believe you are right," blurted Thomas. "Both Dr. Pearson and Dr.—er—Graydon think the stains are blood. Brown is questioning McMinn now."

Just then the local man re-entered and shook his head as he looked at Thomas.

"It wasn't the murderer. McMinn says his hand was wet with blood when he went to the door, when he went to admit Dr. Graydon, and he thinks he must have left the stains."

"H'm! So much for that then, but bear it in mind—bear it in mind. Now let's have the maid in and see what she can tell us.'

As he spoke, Inspector Thomas opened the door leading to the kitchen and called to the servant. She came, shy and hesitant, and her nervousness was not lessened by the inspector's abrupt manner. "Your name?" he snapped.

"Maggie Williams, sir."

"How long have you worked here?"

"Three years, sir."

"Do you know what has happened here this evening?"

"No, sir. I—"

"Never mind that. What time did you go out to-day?"

"About half-past two, sir."

"You say you went to Hampstead?"

"Yes, sir—to spend the day with my sister."

"Was everything just as usual in the house here when you went?"

"Yes, sir."

"Do you know if there had been any difference between your master and mistress?'

"Oh, no, sir. Master and mistress never quarrelled."

"Never! In the three years you have been here do you mean to say they never had a difference of opinion?"

"I never saw it; sir. They were always most affectionate like."

"Um! Did they have many visitors?"

"No, sir. No one ever came to stay, but neighbours often ran in during the day."

"Your master's work kept him away from home at night, I believe?"

"Yes, sir. He left about five in the afternoon, and returned early in the morning."

"From that on your mistress was alone?"

"Yes, sir."

"Did she go out much in the evenings?"

"No, sir, scarcely ever, except on Wednesday evenings to the church meeting."

"What time do you retire?"

"About half-past nine, sir."

"And she?"

"About nine."

"Hum! Well, that will do for now. You had better go to your room and remain there quietly until you are wanted. I may tell you that your mistress has met with a very serious accident, but you need not feel nervous, for a constable will be in the house all night."

The maid looked frightened, but managed to murmur something, and fled. Inspector Thomas turned to the local man.

"You had better get hold of some woman to come here. The body will need to be prepared—inquest and post-mortem to be arranged. I'll come back in the morning. Have everything else left undisturbed."

"Very good, chief. What about McMinn?"

"Nothing for the present. He won't be going to work for a few days, anyway. Keep an eye on him, but don't restrict his movements. I presume Dr. Pearson will look after the necessary medical details. Better get in touch with the coroner to-night. Push things right along. I want to know what it was that killed her. Are you ready, Blake?"

"If you don't mind I'd like to have a look in the different rooms," said Blake. "It won't take long, and things might become disturbed."

"All right; I'll come with you."

So while the local man and the two doctors returned to the sitting-room, Blake, Inspector Thomas, and Tinker began to make a tour of the different rooms. The sitting-room and dining-room they had already seen. The parlour did not detain them long, and from there they proceeded to the little breakfast-room or conservatory at the back.

Blake showed considerable interest as his eyes fell on the double French windows which opened to the garden at the back.

"Have you your flash lamp?" he asked the inspector.

Thomas produced one, and, opening the doors, Blake stood at the head of the short flight of steps.

"I think Inspector Brown said he had already searched the house and grounds?" he remarked.

"Yes; so he said."

"Well, it is to be hoped they have not trampled up the ground too much."

As he spoke Blake bent down and flashed the light on the steps. He worked his way down, one by one, until he came to the gravel at the bottom. He spent some time there before moving on along the path.

A few feet away from the steps the ground suddenly showed damp, and, looking to one side, it was easy enough to see how this had come about, for on one of the flower-beds there was a large watering can where it had been left by someone after watering the plants.

Blake worked his way along towards the bank of the river at the bottom. The inspector followed him closely, but if he found anything to hold his interest Blake did not communicate it to them. When he reached the edge of the bank he paused and switched out the light.

Overhead the stars were very brilliant in the clear summer sky, and, away across the reservoir to the east, a big golden moon was just rising. It gave just sufficient light for them to see along the bank to a little bridge some twenty or thirty yards above them.

Between them and the hedge were several other narrow garden strips, belonging to other villas, and they could see a tiny path which ran along the bank in each direction—a means of going and coming for the reservoir employees. At last the inspector's curiosity got the bettor of him.

"What is it, Blake?" he asked. "What is the big idea?"

Blake smiled to himself in the gloom. "Nothing at all, inspector. I was just curious to see the lay of the place. Since you were good enough to ask me to come along I am trying to take an intelligent interest in things."

Thomas grunted.

"You seem to have no difficulty in doing so, then. From what I know of you, you don't go mooching about like this unless something has caught your eye."

"I have seen nothing that the local inspector could not see," countered Blake. "Frankly, I am very glad you asked me to come along. There are certain features —certain features, inspector—" And then Blake's voice trailed off. "What about a look at the upper rooms?" he asked after a few moments.

"If you wish. But hadn't we better leave that until the morning?"

"Ah! I did not know I should be coming down again."

"Why not? You can't fool me. You know you are already keen to find the answer to this riddle."

Blake laughed.

"Well, we shall see," he rejoined. "I am ready to return if you are."

They made their way back to the house, and were just passing through the hall when John McMinn stumbled out of the sitting-room. Certain sounds from the floor above told Blake that the body of the dead woman had already been carried up, and just then the doorbell rang. Inspector Thomas signed for the constable to answer it, and a middle-aged woman in nurse's uniform was admitted.

It was the woman for whom Inspector Brown had telephoned. Thomas went towards her in order to explain what she had to do, and it was then Sexton Blake felt a touch on his arm. He turned to find John McMinn gazing at him beseechingly.

"I heard them mention your name, sir," he said in a whisper. "You are the famous Mr. Sexton Blake?"

"Sexton Blake is my name," acknowledged Blake.

"Then please, sir, I beg you give me a few moments. I must speak to you."

Wondering somewhat, Blake signed to Tinker to wait, and followed McMinn into the sitting-room As soon as they were away from the door McMinn turned.

"I know what they are thinking, Mr. Blake!" he said hoarsely. "The way they look at me and everything. They think I had something to do with this. But I did not. I am innocent, I swear it. In all the years of our married life there never was a cross word between my wife and me. But they may arrest me and I may be tried. My wife was murdered—I know that. And I want to find the person who killed her. She hadn't an enemy in the world, and that is why they will say I did it, for she had private means of her own, and they may say I was the only one with a motive. But I have saved some money myself, and I will give you every penny of that if you will find the person who killed my wife. You have helped so many people in the past—will you help me in this?"

"But the police are quite competent," rejoined Blake. "Inspector Thomas, of Scotland Yard, is a very able officer, and besides, I think you are allowing your sorrow to make you too emotional. Inspector Brown has a very high opinion of you, and I do not think anyone suspects you of this foul crime."

"Perhaps, and perhaps not. But I shall be helpless to do anything, and the police are so slow. I want the murderer found, Mr. Blake. Will you take the case for me?"

"I'll think it over," said Blake, after a pause. "My visit here was simply made at the invitation of Inspector Thomas. I could not take a professional interest in it unless I first spoke to him. I shall do so, and then let you know."

"Thank you, thank you, Mr. Blake. I—"

But at that moment Inspector Thomas called to Blake, and the latter made a gesture for McMinn to say nothing more. On the way back to London Thomas asked Blake what McMinn had wanted. Blake told him frankly.

"So he thinks he is suspect, does he," muttered Thomas. "Well, I don't mind telling you, Blake, that I am not so sanguine about that bird as the local inspector. I gather that his wife had quite considerable private means, and he had plenty of motive for doing her in. If all we have heard is true, then who else would want to kill her?"

"I haven't an idea," rejoined Blake. "Would you mind if I took a hand in it?"

"Not at all. Glad to have you, as far as I am concerned. But I have a hunch that it is not going to prove as mysterious as it seemed at first. I fancy we will find that McMinn shot her before he went out to post the letter. There is no doubt that it took place at that time, for Dr. Graydon said the body was still warm when he arrived. Rigor had not set in."

"You may be right, but what about the sound of the shot. There were people about the road. McMinn said he spoke to some acquaintances on his way to the pillar-box. It has been a still, quiet evening, and there is little or no traffic in Woodberry Down, for no through traffic goes that way. I happen to know there is a barrier at the end by the bridge, and only pedestrians can pass through."

"Well, it looks as if it was a bullet that had done it. The post-mortem will be to-morrow, and we shall know then. If no one heard the shot, it must have been just a fluke, and the murderer risked it. What you can't get away from is the fact that the woman had lived there for fifteen years, and her life is an open book. She is just like thousands of other people who live a mediocre-life in a quiet suburb. Who on earth would want to kill her if it wasn't her husband? The only other conceivable theory is that a lunatic was abroad."

"There is weight in what you say," mused Blake. Then abruptly: "I wonder if it was generally known that she wore a wig. Until I saw that in the doctor's notes I never should have suspected it. A wig like that would cost a large amount of money. It was made by a master, and I don't know many London hairdressers who could turn out such a perfect bit of work—not even Clarkson, who is a master."

"Well, what about that? The wig can't have anything to do with the murder."

"I didn't say so, but doesn't it strike you as a little odd, that a woman in her sphere of life—a placid type of woman in middle age, living such a humdrum existence, would go to such expense at the dictates of her vanity?"

"'Oh, I don't know. You never know what a woman will do when it comes to her personal appearance. They will chuck money away on all sorts of foolishness just in order to cover up a defect. I don't think that has anything in it."

Blake laughed and drew out a cigar.

"Perhaps you are right," he said pleasantly. "But you haven't answered my question yet."

"I have told you I don't mind in the least. If McMinn can afford to employ you, go ahead. But he won't touch any of his wife's money until I am satisfied about him."

"The question of a fee hadn't occurred to me. I think however, that I'd like to follow up this case. I should like to see how soon you land your man."

The inspector glared at him suspiciously, but made no remark, and a few minutes later they reached Trafalgar Square. Blake and Tinker got out there, for Blake had refused to allow the police car to take them on to Baker Street.

They bade the inspector good-night, making a tentative appointment at the villa in Woodberry Down for the following morning at ten o'clock. Then Blake hailed a taxi, and they got in.

"What do you think about the whole thing, guv'nor?"asked Tinker, as they rattled along. "Why did you mention the wig?"

"I haven't given much thought to it, so far," responded Blake. "And as for the wig—well, my lad, I did not mention it to the inspector, for he is apt to get a little grumpy at times. But on the inside of the wig was a small cross in green silk tape, and I happen to know that green silk cross is the private mark of Jules, the most exclusive and expensive coiffeur in Paris. That wig is a real masterpiece, and couldn't have cost less than ten thousand francs. That is why I was puzzled to find it on the head of a woman who, from what we know, was the wife of a foreman printer, whose earnings could not amount to more than four or five hundred a year at most, and whose whole scheme of life was the direct anthithesis of the clientele who patronise Jules, in the Champs Elysees."

"But they say she had money of her own, guv'nor?"

"Quite so, young 'un, quite so; but Jules—"

And there Blake broke off, for they were just drawing into the kerb in front of the house in Baker Street.

4.   Blake Questions McMinn—The Result of the Post-mortem—An Important Discovery.

BLAKE did not go down to Finsbury Park with Inspector Thomas the next morning. Instead, he sent Tinker round to the garage a few minutes after nine for the Grey Panther, and the two motored down alone.

On reaching the villa—Bruyere Villa, Blake saw by daylight it had been named— they found no signs of the police. In the sitting-room, sunk in an easy-chair in which his wife had died, was John McMinn. He looked as if he hadn't had a wink of sleep all night, but on seeing Sexton Blake he made an effort to pull himself together.

Blake put a few questions, which told him what had occurred since the previous night. The body of the dead woman had been removed for the post-mortem, and the servant would have gone too, but for the stern injunction of Inspector Brown. So much Blake learned before he approached the crux of the matter.

A cold pipe on the table told him that McMinn was a smoker, so he persuaded him to light up. He himself lit an A-Bats-chari cigarette, his favourite morning weed, and when the man was more composed under the influence of the tobacco, he said: "Last night you asked me to help you in this sad affair, Mr. McMinn. Well, I have come down to tell you that I am prepared to do so on one condition."

"What is that condition, sir?"

"That you answer every question I put to you in the fullest manner and with complete truth."

"I have nothing to conceal, sir. I will answer anything you ask me to the best of my ability. Find the scoundrel who killed my wife—that is all I ask."

"How long were you married?"

"Nineteen years—a little over."

"I understood Inspector Brown to say that you have lived here for some fifteen years?"

"That is so."

"Where did you live before that?"

"At Ealing."

"Where were you married?"

"At Ealing."

"How long had you known your wife before you married her?"

"Ever since we were children."

"Did you both live at Ealing before marriage?"

"Yes, sir. I will explain. My wife's family lived there and so did mine. Her people were tradesmen in a good way of business. My father followed the same trade which I follow. At one time he was in business on his own but did not make a success of it. I knew Bertha— my wife— as a child. We went to the same church in Ealing and knew the same circle of friends. We had been sweethearts from ever so young."

"So your wife's whole life was known to you."

"Everything."

"Do you mean that she spent her whole life in Ealing?"

"Yes—or no, not all of it. She went abroad for about a year."

"How did that come about?"

"It was this way. An aunt of hers died and left all her money to Bertha. The old lady was pretty well off and, when the money came to Bertha, her people had ambitions for her. So they sent her abroad for a year—thought she might do better for herself than marrying me, I suppose."

"Where did she go?"

"To Paris."

"With whom did she stay there?"

"She stayed in one of those—what do you call them—pensions."

"Yes, that is right. And she was there a year."

"Yes."

"How old was she when she went?"

"Nineteen or twenty."

"How long after her return were you married?"

"Some years—she was twenty-four."

"That would make her about forty-four now."

"Yes. I am forty-six."

"Did you notice any difference in her when she returned?"

John McMinn was silent for a little then he answered slowly.

"Not exactly, except that she used to get nervous spells, if you know what I mean."

"I think I do. How did these spells affect her?"

"I can't exactly say. She would get moody and refuse to see me for two or three days at a time; then she would be all right."

"Did she ever express a desire to return to Paris?"

"No, sir, never. On the contrary. She always said she hated the place and never wanted to see it again."

"After your marriage—did she ever leave you?"

"No, sir, never!"

"About holidays—did you always take them together?"

"Yes."

"Did you ever leave her—was it ever necessary for you to go away on business?"

"No. Our whole married life has been spent together."

"I notice this villa has a French name. Did you give it that name?"

"Let me think—no, it was my wife. I remember she said the word meant heath or heather, and sounded nice, so I said all right."

"Do you mind telling me when it was that your wife's hair began to go thin?"

"About nine or ten years ago. She had an illness, and it came out then. Ever since that time she has worn a wig."

"I see. Well, McMinn, Inspector Thomas from the Yard will be here before long, but I should like to go over the upstairs rooms before he comes. Will you show me the way or would you rather remain here?"

"I'll come if you wish, Mr. Blake. I'll do anything to help you, and if the inspector is coming, let us hurry."

Blake could have desired nothing better so he rose at once and allowed McMinn to lead the way to the hall. They went up the stairs, and, at the top, McMinn led the way to a room on the right. He opened the door and stood aside.

"This was her room," he said chokingly. "I'll wait outside if you don't mind." Blake paused for a moment.

"Then you didn't occupy the same room?"

"No. My room is the adjoining one. You see I work all night and get home at an early hour in the morning. I didn't want to wake her when I came in so I used a different room."

"Ah, yes! I understand!"

Then Blake entered and stood just within the door, looking round. What he saw was more or less what he expected to see, except that the furniture was undoubtedly solid mahogany of a more massive and more expensive type than one would have looked for in a small semi-detached suburban villa.

There was a big dressing-table, a wide double bed with a gaudy lace counterpane, a huge wardrobe, two heavy tables and some chairs. The curtains were good and so was the carpet.

The pictures were of ordinary subjects, landscapes and two of the seasons, with the exception of one. That one was an engraving from what Blake knew was the frontispiece of an old edition of Dante's Inferno, and he looked at it for several seconds before he turned his gaze away. It was a curious subject to find in a suburban bed-room.

The room itself yielded nothing of any particular interest beyond what one could see on entering. In one corner was a door, and this, Blake found, opened into a deep wall cupboard. He saw that the place was full of feminine garments, and that on the right was a chest of drawers. He had no desire to investigate the dead woman's intimate apparel, but be did pull open the drawers.

In the top one he saw a heap of lingerie. In the second he found some blouses and ribbons. In the third he came upon some furs, redolent of the smell of mothballs. The fourth and last held nothing but a wooden box, painted black and about the size of an ordinary despatch-case.

Blake lifted it out and examined the lock. It did not look a very difficult one so he signed to Tinker to keep a watch through the door to see if McMinn entered the room. Then he took out his bunch of keys, and, after a few moment's scrutiny, chose one. He inserted this in the lock and turned. As he expected the lock yielded readily enough.

He lifted the cover and bent over the contents. Then he lifted his head and set the box down carefully. Watching him closely, Tinker knew that he had found something interesting. And a second or so later the lad saw what it was.

Blake thrust in his hand and lifted out— a beautifully fashioned blonde wig—an exact counterpart of the one which Mrs. McMinn had been wearing when she had been killed.

He turned it over until he could see the lining, and, there in an inconspicuous spot at the top was a small green silk cross of narrow tape. It was the mark of the famous "Jules."

Blake laid the wig aside and again thrust in his hand. He brought it out again, and this time Tinker could not suppress a gasp. Like the other object it was a wig, but this one was not blonde. It was not even brown. It was as black as ebony, and, when he turned it over, Blake again saw a small green silk cross in tape.

He laid this aside, and for the third time his hand went into the box. Out it came once more, and Tinker's astonished gaze took in still another wig of raven black. It too had a small green silk cross sewn at the top of the lining.

Blake canted the box and saw that it contained nothing else. He then replaced the wigs just as he had taken them out, after which he closed the lid and locked it.

As he turned round he laid a warning finger on his lip before signing to the lad to pass out. But as he turned to obey, Tinker could have sworn that he heard Blake murmur:

"Four of them—two blonde, two black— ten thousand apiece at least, and that is forty thousand francs."

They rejoined McMinn in the hall, and from there proceeded to his bed-room. It did not take Blake long to complete his tour of this room, and he found exactly what he expected, which was nothing. Then they examined a spare room, and after that, at the end of a small hall, looked into the servant's room, but did not enter.

Blake said that he would not bother looking into the two attic rooms above, so they descended to the lower floor. There Blake told McMinn to wait in the sitting-room.

"The inspector may be here at any moment," he said. "I just want to have a look in the garden."

He and Tinker passed through the small breakfast-room and down the steps to the garden at the back. By daylight they could see exactly how it lay in relation to the river, the reservoir and the villas on each side.

They walked slowly to the river bank, and, standing there, Blake again turned his gaze towards the little bridge some fifty yards or so away.

"Let us walk along the path, my lad," he said.

They proceeded slowly, ignoring the numerous tell-tale movements of curtains in the back windows of the houses which they passed, and from time to time Blake would stop and gaze intently at the soft ground.

They proceeded in this way until they had almost reached the bridge; then Blake turned back.

"The inspector should be here," he said.

"He will probably be none too pleased that we came down before him so let us make our peace. I have seen all I want to see anyway, but I am anxious to know the result of the post-mortem. We should be able to get that soon now."

He had judged his time well, for no sooner did they enter the house than they saw Inspector Thomas standing in the hall.

"I thought you were coming down with me," he bellowed at sight of them. "I telephoned to Baker Street and couldn't get an answer."

Blake smiled.

"Since I made up my mind to take the case on behalf of Mr. McMinn I didn't think it quite fair to make use of your car," he answered easily. "We haven't been here long—just been having a look round. Heard anything of the result of the post-mortem yet?"

"No. Ought to hear anytime on such a simple job. Dr. Pearson and our own pathologist are at it now."

"Well, I don't think I shall wait. I'd be grateful, though, if you would give me a note to Dr. Pearson. I could drop in on the way and find out the result, if it is known.

"I only came on here to see if you were here. We can drive back together. Come in my car and Tinker can drive yours after us."

"All right."

Blake went into the sitting-room to speak to McMinn.

"I am taking this case as I told you," he said, laying his hand on the man's shoulder. "Don't you worry about the police or about fees. Answer every question the police may put to you. Keep nothing back. As soon as I find it necessary to talk with you again I shall either come here or telephone you. But don't forget—if you don't hear from me for a few days that does not mean I am not busy. And I don't think you need worry about arrest just yet."

The man tried to thank him, but Blake brushed that aside. He followed the inspector out to the police car and climbed in. Tinker took the wheel of the Grey Panther and the two cars relied along up Woodberry Down.

Ten minutes later they were in conversation with Dr. Pearson and the pathologist. The former was holding a small object between his finger and thumb, and Blake and the inspector were listening attentively while he was saying:

"It is just as we thought—a bullet did it. She was killed by this bit of lead, discharged from a pistol which could not have been held more than a dozen feet or so away from where she was sitting."

Blake's mind went back quickly to the sitting-room. He had

already taken good care to figure what line of flight the bullet must have taken.

He knew from the position of the easy-chair how the woman must have been sitting, and he had already concluded that, if it had been a bullet that had entered the heart, then it must have come from a weapon held by someone who was standing just inside the door of the room.

He waited until the inspector had examined the bullet.

"Thirty-eight calibre," he grunted as he passed it to Blake.

Blake examined it closely before he handed it back. He made no comment whatsoever, and a few minutes later, leaving the inspector with the two doctors, he returned to the Grey Panther.

He got in beside Tinker and told the lad to drive back to Baker Street.

"What was the verdict?" asked Tinker, curiously, as he sent the Grey Panther at high speed along the Seven Sisters Road.

"What we thought—a bullet in the heart. It is one of .38 calibre."

"Huh! That takes a pretty hefty weapon, guv'nor. Isn't it rather funny that no one heard the sound of the shot? Have the police made inquiries next door?"

"I understood Inspector Thomas to say that the people who live next door had been questioned, but had heard nothing. But I am not at all surprised."

"Why, guv'nor?"

"Because, young 'un, there was little or no noise to hear. The bullet was fired from a weapon of .38 calibre all right; but it is not what one would classify as an ordinary bullet. There is a peculiar glassy surface to the bullet which the inspector has missed for the moment. But I happened to notice it.

"The bullet, in my opinion, is of a type which I have seen in Italy and, my experience of that type has been that they are almost entirely manufactured for use in a very powerful description of Italian pistol which is discharged by compressed air. Hence—no noise."

5. A Visit to Paris—Jules, the Wig-maker—Trailed to London.

ON their return to Baker Street, Blake sat down and, as was his custom, when he had started on a new case, dictated to Tinker a mass of preliminary notes. As he went along Tinker, knowing by now pretty well how Blake's mind worked, could read a good deal of the story which those notes told and always, when he had finished, it was his custom to ask Blake questions about them—a thing which Blake encouraged for, besides exercising the lad's own mind, it helped him to adjust the various items in their correct perspective.

And on this occasion Tinker followed his usual course.

"I get the hang of what you have dictated, guv'nor," he said as he pushed the shorthand book aside, "but I don't quite follow that business about the back garden. Do you think the murderer came that way?"

"I am almost certain of it, my lad."

"But how do you make that out, sir?"

"It was the only way for him to come— if we eliminate John McMinn. You saw the path at the bottom of the garden which runs along the bank of the stream."

"Yes, guv'nor, but—"

"Wait a moment. You also noticed, I presume, the fairly high hedge which runs at the back of the villas adjoining?"

"Of course."

"And you saw the bridge?"

"Yes, sir."

"Well, that is it—too easy. The murderer came that way. He climbed down over the bridge, sneaked along the path on the bank, bending, possibly to keep himself concealed behind the hedge, and simply walked up the McMinn's garden. He entered the house through the small room at the back. From there it was only a few steps along the hall to the door of the sitting-room. He pushed that open, saw the woman sitting in the chair by the window, raised his weapon and fired. Then he simply returned the way he had come."

"But—but how did he know when to enter, guv'nor?"

"He didn't most likely. He took a chance on that. He may have been lurking in the house for some little time, or he may have come in at just the opportune moment. At any rate, he was there when McMinn went to post his letter. And in those few minutes he succeeded in carrying out his purpose."

"Then you don't think McMinn did it?"

"Not a chance! The man is as innocent as you or I. He was genuinely fond of his wife."

"But who could do such a thing? From all I can gather from what has been said and these notes, no one could have a motive for killing her."

"Someone did, my lad—and a very strong one at that. I will even go so far as to say that the person was possibly an undersized man of slight build, a foreigner— possibly French or Italian."

"Scott, guv'nor, how do you make that out?"

"By perfectly plain footmarks in the garden and along the path beside the stream. Last night, when Inspector Thomas kindly lent me his torch, I saw damp marks on the steps. The person who had left those had been on those steps within a very short time. I found the same prints in the damp part of the path, near where the watering-can had been left. Those same marks were to be seen this morning when we walked along the path. They were undersized for a man, and oversize for any but a big woman. Had they been made by a big woman, they would have been deeper; hence, I say they were made by an undersized man."

"But why a foreigner?"

"Because the heels were of a foreign shape. They were of the type known in this country as 'Cuban,' and very few Englishmen wear them. But they are common on the Continent."

"Whew! That's going some, guv'nor. But what about the motive. Nothing was said about anything of value being missing, and I remember I saw her rings on her fingers."

"Quite right. Robbery was not the motive. I have already said that the motive was a very strong one, but I don't know yet what it was."

"What about those wigs, guv'nor? That was a funny collection. She must have been a queer duck to wear black ones and blonde ones, too."

"You have touched on the very point which is going to have our next attention, Tinker. Those wigs, in my opinion, hold something very close to the secret of why this quiet-living woman in that villa was shot down in cold blood. In all the record of her life which I have received, I can find only one occasion when she even ventured as far abroad as Paris. That was more than twenty years ago, and so far it is the only thing that in any way connects her with a foreign country. Ever since then she has lived a most humdrum life—as far as we know."

"What is the next step then, sir?"

"I am going to run over to Paris, my lad. I am going to leave you here, for I want you to keep in touch with things as they progress. The inquest will be held to-morrow, and I want you to be there. You will listen carefully to all the evidence, and take shorthand notes, for my examination when I return. I am going to try and find out why this woman should have such an inordinate vanity as to buy her wigs from the most exclusive and expensive hairdresser in all Europe."

At that Blake rose, and Tinker knew it would be of no use questioning him further then. He knew what Blake would require for a short journey to Paris, so he packed a bag for his master, and that afternoon drove him to Victoria, to catch the afternoon train.

Blake had made no definite plans as to how he should approach Jules. He knew that the coiffeur would have to be handled tactfully if he were to get anything out of him, for Blake knew enough of the breed to realise that the man would have an entirely exaggerated idea of his own importance in the scheme of things.

Jules, like the more famous Marcel, had discovered a method of hair waving which had become the rage. He had kept the real secret of it to himself, only allowing his numerous assistants to do the preliminary work, so to speak.

Hence it can be understood that he was literally besieged by fashionable women, and such a pinnacle had he reached that he could pick and choose his clientele from the very cream of the haute monde.

Little wonder is it, therefore, that Sexton Blake was amazed to find, not one, but four of "Jules'" masterpieces in the private box of a very ordinary woman in a London suburb.

And it was no small piece of work to make one of those wigs. He might be a robber—which he was—but at the same time "Jules" was a master of his craft, and he stood supreme as the master wig-maker of Europe. Ten thousand francs for one wig— not a sou less—and it was quite likely that the price might be much more.

Yet Mrs. McMinn, wife of a foreman printer, possessed four such wigs! What was the answer to that mystery? That was what Sexton Blake had gone to Paris to try and discover.

He reached the Gare du Nord about half-past ten at night, and drove straight to the Carlitz Hotel, in the Rue de Rivoli, where he was fortunate enough to secure his usual suite. He knew he could do nothing that night, so he did not waste any brain-matter over the business. Instead, he had a nightcap, and then turned in.

But in the morning Blake was astir early. When he had bathed and dressed, he rang for his coffee, and then, lighting a cigarette, he descended to the famous mezzanine floor.

He made his way along there until he came to the rooms given over to the hotel hairdressing-rooms, and, on entering, found, as he had hoped, Monsieur Maurice, who knew Blake as an old and valued client of the Carlitz. He greeted the Englishman profusely, and made to attend on him personally; but Blake smiled, and shook is head.

"Not this morning, Monsieur Maurice," he said. "I came to pay you a personal visit. Is there any place where we can talk privately?"

"But yes, Monsieur Blake. Will you do me the honour to come to my private bureau?"

Blake followed him into a snug little office, where Maurice ensconced him in a comfortable easy-chair. He then closed the door, and looked at Blake inquiringly. Blake offered him a cigarette, but the Frenchman shook his head.

"I beg you to excuse me, Monsieur Blake. It is only in the evenings I permit myself to smoke. I must consider my fair clients. The smell of the smoke on one's fingers might be offensive."

Blake understood, and took a mental note at the time of this little point. One could never tell when a little thing like that might come in useful, and he had never thought of it before.

"As you will, monsieur. But do sit down. I wish to ask you one or two questions." When the Frenchman had done so, Blake went on:

"You know Monsieur Jules, who has his establishment up the Champs Elysees?"

"But yes, monsieur, I know him well."

"He is a—friend of yours?"

"Not a friend, monsieur—an acquaintance. We are in the same profession."

"Quite so. Er—I am very anxious to gain a little information, Monsieur Maurice, which can only be secured through that establishment. Can you help me?"

"It depends, monsieur," came the answer slowly. "I know that you are in a certain profession, Monsieur Blake, and that you have done many valuable services for this hotel. But it is a delicate thing which you ask. Jules is tres difficile, if I may say so."

"This should not be difficult. For some years Jules has been making wigs for a certain person in England—in London. I am anxious, if possible, to find out what records he has on his books regarding that client. I have reason to believe that she never comes to Paris, so the wigs must be made from a standing model."

"Ah! That is not so serious, monsieur. Let me think, please."

The Frenchman leant his head on his hands and went into a brown study. He remained motionless for some minutes; then suddenly he lifted his head and jumped up.

"Excuse me, monsieur," he said quickly. "I have an idea. I shall return in a few minutes."

He left the room, and Blake sat waiting. Fully a quarter of an hour passed before Maurice returned, but, when he did, Blake saw that he was smiling.

"It is arranged, monsieur, if monsieur is willing to pay a trifling price for the service."

"Most certainly—any figure you care to name."

"It will not be much. I have an assistant here. His brother is employed at Jules. He says, that if monsieur cares to pay, he will see his brother this morning and get him to find out what monsieur wants to know."

"Good—excellent. I am indebted to you, Monsieur Maurice. I will write down in French exactly what I desire to find out."

Forthwith Blake began writing. He gave a very careful description of the black wigs and the blonde wigs which he had seen at the villa in Finsbury Park, and this he handed to Maurice. The latter took it, read it, then, with a nod, he disappeared.

He came back a little time after to announce that he had given his assistant special leave for the morning, and that he had already started off on his errand. Then Blake switched the conversation back to Jules.

"What sort of a man is Jules?" he asked. "I mean, in his appearance."

Maurice shrugged.

"He is *petit.* Monsieur Blake—a small man."

"How old is he?"

Again the Frenchman shrugged.

"Who can say? Perhaps he is forty, perhaps five years more."

"Is he fair or dark?"

"He would be white, monsieur, but he dyes his hair a raven black."

"A smallish man—dyed hair," murmured Blake. Then, aloud: "Thank you, monsieur. When your assistant returns, would you please let me know? I think what I shall give him for his trouble will satisfy him."

"I shall send word to monsieur's room the instant he comes back."

"Thank you."

With that, Blake took his departure, and, since he had nothing else to do for the time being, he went for a walk. He strolled up the Champs Elysees until he saw Jules' establishment on the opposite side of the avenue. He studied it out of the corner of his eye, but he did not pause.

He carried on until he came to the Etoile, then he retraced his steps, and he had scarcely reached his sitting-room when the table telephone rang. He lifted the receiver and recognised the voice of the hairdresser at the other end of the wire.

"Ah, monsieur, it is twice that I have called you! Have I your permission to come up?"

"By all means. I am sorry I did not return sooner."

Within a few minutes there was a knock at the door, and at his command it opened to admit Maurice. He closed it after him and advanced, a piece of paper in his hand.

"Monsieur, my assistant has returned; but I regret that he was unable to discover very much. He did succeed in finding out that a client in England receives wigs of the exact type which monsieur described, but they are not sent in the ordinary way. The name on the books is down simply as 'Madame Berthe.'

"The records show that the wigs are supplied once every two years—one blonde and one black at the same time. They are made against a standing order, and a special messenger from London comes over to take them across.

"Nor is there any record in the books that any payment is received for them. That is all, but there can be not the slightest doubt that they are the wigs to which monsieur referred."

Blake listened in silence to what the hairdresser said. When he had finished, he nodded.

"I am extremely grateful to you, Monsieur Maurice. I shall be obliged if you will give this two hundred francs to your assistant. He has given me information which may prove useful."

"But it is too much, monsieur. Two hundred francs! Fifty will be quite sufficient."

But Blake would not listen to him, and forced him to take the two notes which he was holding out. The Frenchman took them reluctantly, and was about to bow and retire, when suddenly he paused.

"I know not monsieur's reason for asking about these wigs, but there is one little thing that may interest monsieur."

"What is that?"

"It seems that Jules is in a very agitated state this morning. A telegram came at an early hour. What it contained I know not, but after reading it Jules grew very excited. He has cancelled all his appointments for some days ahead, and has announced that he is leaving for London this very day."

Blake came to his feet.

"Jules leaving for London! Monsieur Maurice, that is the most interesting news you could have told me. He has not yet left?"

"I believe not, monsieur. He is to take his departure this afternoon, I understand."

"Thank you, monsieur—a thousand thanks."

Maurice bowed himself out, and Sexton Blake closed the door after him. He walked to the table and stood drumming his fingers on it.

"So I was right about the wigs," he muttered. "A blonde one and a black one made against a standing order every two years. No record of any payment being made for them, and they are taken to London by a special messenger who comes over for them. It gets more and more mysterious. Why is it that a suburban dweller in London receives such consideration from the haughty Jules? Why no payment? Why the special messenger? It is the sort of consideration that would only be given to royalty or someone closely approaching it. And yet that fat, placid woman in that semi-detached villa in Finsbury Park received that sort of treatment. Why? What the deuce had Jules, the hairdresser of the Champs Elysees, to do with her? Is it possible—is it conceivable that there is some secret link here that connects up with that time when she was in Paris more than twenty years ago? If so, then what is the meaning of it all?

"How could she live a quiet, humdrum life all those years without a single thing cropping up? If she had ever gone away from home alone, one could imagine that might be so. But she never did. In nineteen years of married life she was never away from her husband. She has spent those years in Ealing and in Finsbury Park. I cannot recall ever having come upon a more mysterious or curious case. What can be the meaning of it?"

"And now—this morning—Jules receives a telegram which throws him into a state of great excitement. What was in that telegram? Did it come from London? If so, did it contain the news of that woman's death? And if it did, who sent it? Whatever it was—whomsoever sent it—Jules is off to London to-day. And by whichever train he travels, I travel, too.

"I think I shall find that same young assistant useful in pointing out my man to me on the station. If he leaves this afternoon, it means he must travel by the four o'clock from the Gare du Nord. If not then, it will be the eight forty-five from the Gare St. Lazare. I'll see Maurice again."

With that he left the room and made his way once more to the mezzanine floor. Maurice was only too pleased to accommodate him, and the young assistant only too happy to be of use to the generous patron who had sent him two hundred francs for a very simple service.

After that, Blake lunched in the grillroom and left in a taxi in good time for the Gare du Nord. He was accompanied by the young assistant; who took up a position of vantage on the platform from where he could watch everyone who came through the gates.

Blake was standing at one side reading, so that the journal covered his face, and it was not until the young man touched his arm that he knew something of interest was taking place.

"It is he, monsieur," he whispered. "That man, with the black soft hat and the grey coat. Yes, yes, monsieur, just stepping into the carriage."

"Good! I have him now," returned Blake. "You need not stay longer. I do not want you to be seen. Here, monsieur, take this note and my deep thanks."

"Merci, monsieur. You are too generous."

He sped away then, and Blake leisurely sought a place. He knew that he need not watch his man too closely, for it was obvious that he was travelling to London, and Blake did not want to rouse his suspicions.

So he contented himself with keeping an eye on him at Calais and again at Dover, and from the latter place he sent a telegram to Tinker.

On arriving at Victoria he saw the Grey Panther standing on the rank among a lot of other cars and taxis. He had warned the lad in his telegram to remain in the car until he signalled to him, and it was not until he saw Jules enter a taxi and drive off that he gave the sign.

Tinker pulled out of the rank at once, and as he drew alongside the platform Blake leant over and jerked:

"That taxi just ahead. Follow it and find out where the occupant is dropped. I shall go on to Baker Street in a taxi. But don't you lose that trail, even if you have to leave the Grey Panther standing."

Tinker nodded his understanding, and was off just as the taxi disappeared through the gates.

Blake had no fear that the lad would stick to his quarry, so he signalled to a taxi, and was soon on his way to Baker Street.

He settled down to work almost at once, for there were already arrears to make up, and he was still at it some two hours later when Tinker came in.

"Well?" queried Blake curtly.

"I followed him all right, guv'nor. The taxi drove to Chelsea—to a big house in Church Street. I marked it down all right. The fare got out there and paid off the taxi. He then entered the house, carrying his bag with him, and the taxi drove off. I stuck round for a bit to see if he would come out, but he did not do so, so I thought the best thing to do was to come on here and report."

"Quite right, my lad. A house in Church Street, Chelsea. Do you know the place?"

"I've seen it before, guv'nor, but I don't know anything about it. It is a very old house—looks as if it might have been there when Chelsea was still in the country. There are quite considerable grounds around it and a high wall. It is a gloomy-looking hole."

"What is the number?"

"Number 182A."

"I can't place it. Let me see—I have it! Get through on the 'phone to special agent X093—that is in his territory —tell him what you have told me, and instruct him to get all the data about the place that he can. Tell him I want him to report here this evening if possible. When you have done that let me have the notes you made at the inquest."

6.   The Strange Connection of Madame Berthe with Jules the Coiffeur—The House in Chelsea and Chinese Joint in Limehouse.

BLAKE and Tinker had just finished dinner that evening, and were sitting in the consulting-room talking in desultory fashion, when the bell sounded. A few minutes later Mrs. Bardell knocked and entered. She handed Blake a small white card on which some cryptic letters had been pencilled, and, as he saw them, Blake turned to the housekeeper.

"Show him in, please," he said.

Mrs. Bardell retired, and a few moments later the door opened again. In shuffled an extraordinary looking person. He was an undersized little gutter rat of indeterminate age. He might have been anything from forty to sixty.

His clothes were old and quite filthy. His face hadn't seen a razor for many days, while his hair was unkempt and gagged. His eyes were bleary and furtive and bold at the same time. His face was patchy, red and purple and streaky white—the face of a confirmed drinker, or, rather, drunkard. His boots were old and out at toe. In his hand he twirled a greasy cap.

He made an awkward bow to Blake, and then to Tinker. In fact, he grinned at the lad, exhibiting the stump of one tooth as he did so. It was Tinker who had discovered him selling papers in front of a certain public house in the King's Road in Chelsea, and, after a close study of the rat, had persuaded Blake to enroll him among the growing army of secret agents which was becoming such an integral part of his organisation.

He was known as special agent X093, and it was this person to whom Tinker had telephoned instructions.

Blake tossed him over a cigar, but did not ask him to sit down. When the rat had mangled the end in a way that made Blake shudder, the detective said:

"You have something to report?"

"Yes, sir. I got the message all right. I couldn't go at once until I found someone to take my papers. But I wasn't long delayed. I went to Church Street and found the house. Then I went to a friend of mine who works in a pub close by there. He knew quite a lot about it."

"What did he tell you?"

"Well, sir, it's a queer sort of place. It's one of them bridge clubs as they call them. Leastwise, it is licensed as that. But from what I can hear there isn't much of that sort of thing goes on there."

"What do you mean? What goes on there?"

"I don't know, and he don't know. But it's a shady place, guv'nor. There is a steady lot of people goes there, and they are mostly foreigners. My friend don't rightly know what they do, but there are rumours about it. As far as I can make out I should say it is a gambling den of a different sort."

"Um! Who runs it? Do you know?"

"I saw another party about that—friend of mine whose name I can't mention. He knows more about it. The place is known among certain persons as Madame Berthe's. But nobody ain't ever seen her, it seems, although this friend of mine says she is there all right."

Blake sat up with a jerk.

"Are you sure of that?"

"Certain, guv'nor. I don't ever pass on the information until I know for sure. You can depend that what my friend told me is a fact."

"A gambling den," mused. Blake. "It seems that this place might prove worth investigating. Anything else?"

The rat shifted.

"Well, gnv'nor, this friend of mine told me something else, but I don't know whether it is true."

"What was it?" asked Blake sharply.

The rat stepped forward until he was close to Blake. The latter's nostrils twitched in distaste as he got a whiff of the odour of the rat's unwashed body, but he did not draw back.

Then the rat bent down and whispered something in his ear. As Blake heard, the words his body stiffened and his eyes grew hard. He stared straight into the bleary eyes of the rat.

"Is that on the level?"

"'That's what he says, guv'nor."

"In that case—in that case—well, no more now. But I want you to try and confirm that. If it is that sort of clearing house— I wonder how I could get in there? I suppose the habitues have a countersign?"

"I asked about that, guv'nor. My friend can fix it—for a price."

"You are certain?"

"You can trust him, sir; he is dead safe."

"How can he work it?"

The rat leant over Blake and took a sheet of plain paper. He dragged a short stub of pencil from his pocket and wrote a name and address on it. As Blake read it his brows rose in amazement. It was the name of a notorious Chinese dope dealer in Chinatown, one Willie Chang, whose place both Blake and Tinker knew quite well.

What had Willie Chang of Limehouse to do with that mysterious house in Chelsea? What had "Jules," the exclusive coiffeur of the Champs Elysees, to do with it, and how could Jules be linked up with Willie Chang?

Who was the Madame Berthe who was the tenant of the house in Church Street? Was it just a curious coincidence that her name was the same as that of the woman who had been killed two nights before in the villa at Finsbury Park? If not, what connection was there between those two women—if any?

The more Blake delved into things the more confused did everything become. From the gloom of a quite mediocre suburban household, he had plunged into a stream that began to widen and widen with an ever-growing current.

The green silk crosses in the linings of those wigs had started him off, and, now, within a space of a little over twenty-four hours, he had found the trail of the crosses to lead him to Paris, thence back to Chelsea and now to Willie Chang.

What was the meaning of it all? Was the whole issue becoming confused? And was he becoming sidetracked from the main issue?

He looked up at the rat.

"Willie Chang will not be disposed to welcome me," he said. "He knows that I will kill his vile business if I can."

"He need not know who you are, guv'nor."

"Um! A disguise—yes, that could be done. But how to get to him?"

"My friend will take you, sir, for a price."

"And you say Willie Chang can get me into this house in Chelsea?"

"Dead certain, guv'nor."

"When could your friend take me to Chang?"

"To-night, if you say so, guv'nor,"

"Then let it be to-night. There is no time to waste. What time can he be here?"

"I can see him at once. How would midnight suit you, sir?"

"All right. What about Tinker? I suppose he can come, too."

"I think that would be all right."

"Very well. Tell your friend to be here as close to midnight as possible. I shall pay him a satisfactory fee."

"And a guarantee that he won't run foul of the police? There are one or two little jobs outstanding against him."

"Certainly—I can promise that."

"Very well, guv'nor, he'll be here. The man who comes will just give the word Chelsea as a password, and you'll know I sent him."

"Good!" Then Blake turned to Tinker. "Give this agent twenty pounds, my lad." Tinker jumped up and, whirling the combination of the safe, opened a drawer in the inner compartment. He took out a thick packet of Treasury notes, off which he counted twenty. These he handed to the rat, who took them and, with the speed of a magician, caused them to disappear somewhere beneath his ragged garments. Then he bobbed to each and shuffled out.

When he heard the slam of the street door Blake jumped up and opened one of the windows. Then he lit a cigarette, one of the strongest he possessed.

"Your choice of agents may be a good one, my lad," he grunted, "but I do wish you could persuade some of them to wash occasionally. That one was about the last limit."

He rose.

"Come on, my lad. It is time we fixed up a disguise."

"What about me, guv'nor?"

Blake surveyed him speculatively.

"Um! Let me see. What about a young Italian? That outfit you used in Rome ought to fit the case, I think."

"All right, sir. It won't take me long. And you?"

"I—an Eurasian," answered Blake. "Willie Chang may be all right in this instance, but we can't afford to take any chances."

Each went to his room, then. Tinker dragged out the outfit Blake had suggested, and set to work on his face.

In his dressing-room Blake was also busy. The disguise he had decided to adopt—that of an Eurasian—was one of the safest but, at the same time, most difficult. The chief work lay in broadening his nostrils to just the right degree, and this he accomplished by inserting a small rubber ring in each.

That first step made an extraordinary change in his full face appearance, as well as in his profile, and, when he had greased and then darkened his skin, he began to assume in a remarkable degree the characteristics of the type he had chosen to impersonate.

The clothes he chose were of a tight-fitting style, rather flashy in cut, and just what a fairly well-to-do Eurasian would have worn. With the donning of the garments he altered his ordinary carriage, adopting a slight stoop and a slackness of jaw that gave the last perfect touch.

He slipped a small automatic in his hip-pocket before leaving the room, and stuffed a fairly thick roll of notes in an inner pocket. Then he went to look for Tinker.

He found the lad in the consulting-room and, as he noted each detail of his disguise, he nodded approvingly. For all the world Tinker looked like a greasy Italian youth, such as one may see in any part of Italy and even in the Italian colony in London or New York.

It was easy enough for Tinker to put on the manner and talk with it, for, in his youthful experience of London street life, he had mixed more than a little with "dago" street urchins.

They still had some time to wait, and so they settled down to work until their man should show up.

He came at exactly midnight, and as he entered the consulting-room Blake shot a quick look at Tinker, for he had recognised the friend of the rat as one of the slickest pickpockets in the whole of London.

But the smooth-looking young fellow was quite nonchalant. He looked at Blake with a grin, and then surveyed Tinker. Suddenly he spoke.

"Chelsea," he announced cryptically.

"Chelsea it is," responded Blake. "Are you ready?"

"Yes—but isn't there something to discuss first?"

"You mean terms."

"Sure I mean terms."

"I am ready to talk. How much do you want?"

"You understand that if Chang gets to know the truth it isn't going to be easy for me. He will say I am working with the bulls, and I ain't no stool pigeon. I don't want to wake up with a knife between my ribs."

"I take all that into account. How much do you want?"

"What about a pony?"

"I will pay that, and if things go all right I'll pay two ponies. I'll give you one before we start."

"That's fair enough, guv'nor. I'll play square. But I trust you not to let Willie Chang suspect the truth. I wouldn't do this for anyone else, and I wouldn't do it for you if Jimmie didn't say it was all right."

Blake counted out twenty-five pounds in notes and handed them to the other.

"You will find those right," he said. "Tell me—have you ever seen either of us before?"

"I've seen you, but not the young 'un."

"Do you think our disguises will pass?"

The pickpocket laughed.

"Pass! I should say they will. If I hadn't known what to expect, and if I hadn't got the full strength from Jimmie. I'd have bolted as soon as I laid eyes on you. You look about as much like Sexton Blake as I do."

"Very well—let's go. We can get a taxi along the street. I leave the rest of it to you."

They walked along Baker Street towards Oxford Street, and found a taxi crawling along the kerb in Orchard Street. They hailed it, and the pickpocket gave the man an address in Limehouse.

The man demurred at first, but Blake intervened and told him his tip would he sufficient to reimburse him for a drive to the East End at that hour of the night. Then they got in, and the taxi started off.

It travelled at a rapid pace citywards until they reached the Batik. From there it rolled up Cornhill and into Aldgate. From Aldgate it swung into the Commercial Road, and thence into the murky purlieus of Limehouse.

It twisted through street after street there until it entered a narrow, gloomy cul-de-sac, at one end of which Blake knew Willie Chang's joint was situated. They got out a little way up the street, but before walking on, Blake slipped the driver an extra note.

"Wait here for an hour," he said. "If I don't come by then, don't bother to stay longer. But if you do wait there is another note for you."

"I don't like the place, guv'nor, but I'll stick," answered the man.

They walked along until they reached the last house on the left of the cul-de-sac. At the end was a high wall, and Blake knew that on the other side of that wall was a canal. He had a suspicion that a good many of Willie Chang's clients came and went, by that canal rather than by the streets.

The pickpocket gave a peculiar rap on the door, and presently it was openetl by a young Chinaman. A short colloquy took place between him and the pickpocket, after which the Chink surveyed Blake and Tinker. Then he backed up and allowed them to enter.

They passed through a sort of lobby, then past another door, and found themselves in a bare hall. The Chink left them there while he went to fetch someone else.

Presently the door on the right opened, and Blake saw the notorious Willie Chang come out. He was dressed as a European, in a dinner jacket, and was smoking a cigarette. Willie Chang might deal in opium and "snow," but he took good care not to indulge in any of his own wares.

He nodded to the pickpocket, and then scrutinised Blake and Tinker. He turned back to the pickpocket, and in perfect English, said:

"You vouch for them?"

"Of course. Why do you suppose I brought them."

"What do they want?"

"Oh, a look round; a little game, perhaps, and probably other things."

"All right. If they are not all right, you look out for yourself."

"Don't you threaten me. I've brought many a customer to you, and you know it. What do you take me for, anyway, you yellow skunk."

Willie Chang was quite unperturbed at the insult.

"All right, all right," he said easily. "I am just warning you. Come on."

He led them through the door by which he had entered the hall. They found themselves in a small, bare room, and from this they passed into a short corridor, which seemed to run towards the back. At the end of that Willie Chang opened another door, and they stepped directly into the main gaming-room.

They paused just inside for a few moments, watching the groups about the half-dozen fan-tan and faro tables. Then as the crowd at one table shifted Blake could scarcely restrain a start, for his gaze was resting full on Jules, the exclusive coiffeur of the Champs Elysees.

7. Sexton Blake Gets Into Willie Chang's Haunt —Playing a Desperate Game.

SEXTON BLAKE had heard hints dropped from time to time by certain denizens of the underworld that Willie Chang had slipped back into England since he had been deported some months before. As far as he knew, Scotland Yard were not aware of this and, of course, it had been no part of his duty to pass the tip on.

All the information that came to him through his agents and friends in the underworld, Blake kept to himself until it should prove useful. Had he not observed this caution, the wide-spread system of espionage which it had taken him a score of years to build up, would have been shot to pieces in no time.

He had heard, too, that the Chinaman was back at his old game of peddling dope, he had no actual proof of that, nor, until the visit of the little newspaper rat that evening, had he any idea where Willie Chang's present joint might be located.

All he knew for a fact was that Willie Chang and his brother, the even more notorious Brilliant Chang, no longer conducted their vile traffic from the restaurant in the West End, where they had originally been arrested.

He knew that, of all races, it would be easier for a Chinaman to return to England than any other. To the uninitiated there was an extraordinary sameness in the celestial caste of countenance and, it is only when one has actually lived among them for a considerable time, that one discovers the individual to be quite as marked among Europeans. Alternatively the Chinese, at first, find the same similarity among the western races.

And it was because he knew his East as well as he knew his West that Sexton Blake soon discovered Willie Chang. He had seen the dope peddler several times in the past and, indeed, it was some information which Blake had supplied about the restaurant in the West End that had placed the last link of necessary evidence in the hands of Inspector Thomas to enable him to effect the arrest.

But he was not surprised to find that the Chinaman was much changed in appearance. Not that he had made the mistake of adopting any extreme disguise. He had, as Blake saw at once as soon as he spotted him, trusted to the European penchant for looking upon all Chinese as similar in appearance, more or less, and he had simply made up his face in a manner that added a full score of years to his appearance.

As he was there in that den in Limehouse he could have slithered past any man at the Yard without the slightest risk of being recognised as Willie Chang.

But with Sexton Blake it was different. He knew that Willie Chang was actually back in England—or was almost certain of that—he had been informed that the place to which they were going that evening was Chang's, and he knew every phase of Chinese methods of disguise. He had had to use them himself on many an occasion in the past.

A French hairdresser and a Chinese coast mongrel! A queer pair of birds, that! And yet Sexton Blake was becoming more and more convinced that one of that pair, or both, could tell who had killed the wife of the foreman printer in a London suburb.

Somewhere, somehow, there was a connection. So far he hadn't even the ghost of a suspicion as to what it could be. But it did exist, he was positive, and he was determined that before he finished he should find the answer to the riddle.

He did not think that was going to be easy; nor was it, for it was one of the strangest cases which had ever come his way as Blake was to realise before he reached the end. And that end was to be as bizarre and startling as one could dream of.

He saw that Willie Chang was hovering about in the vicinity of the faro table beside which Jules was standing. He did not walk towards them, but allowed the pickpocket to conduct him and Tinker along to another faro table, a little distance away.

There they took up a position, and began to stake modestly, Tinker and the pickpocket because they were waiting for a lead from Blake, and the latter because he wanted to get some idea of the "layout" of the joint before going further.

The room where the gambling was taking place had been, at one time, he could see, either two or three smaller rooms. The partitions had been knocked out, and now the apartment occupied all the front and the middle of the ground floor. At the rear there were two doors—one in the right-hand corner, and the other in the left. The walls were bare and dirty, the plaster being pitted with holes, as if it had evidently existed for some time. The floor had no rugs, and the chairs were of the plainest deal possible.

There was not the slightest attempt at luxury of fittings and, it was plain to Blake, that Willie Chang had furnished the joint with two purposes in view—one so that he could make a quick getaway, if necessary, without leaving anything of value behind; the other, to supply the bare furnishings needful, so that only those genuinely in want of a real gamble would come.

From the type of house Blake concluded that one of the doors at the back would lead to the rear rooms, and the other, possibly, to a staircase. It was the latter which interested him most.

He did not believe that for a single moment that Chang would confine his activities to gambling. He opined that the Chinaman would have lost no time in getting back into the dope game; but whether he would risk allowing any opium smoking on the premises or not Blake couldn't tell yet.

He had little doubt, however, that a good deal of "snow" and other drugs would be cleared from there, and he kept a sharp eye on the two doors to see if there were any signs of customers passing through.

Chang and Jules remained at the faro table for some considerable time; but at last the Chinaman moved away and after perambulating the room slowly, finally brought up near the door in the left-hand corner. He hovered about there for a few moments then suddenly, he whipped open the door and disappeared.

Blake saw that Jules had also moved away from the faro table, and was taking almost the same course followed by Chang. He, too, reached the corner eventually and, after the fashion of Chang, disappeared swiftly.

Sexton Blake would have given a good deal just then to be able to follow them. But as he couldn't he touched the pickpocket on the arm.

He signed for Tinker to remain at the table. He moved casually away until he and the crook were standing a little apart. Blake took out a cigarette, and while they lit up he murmured:

"The pair who interest me have just gone through that door. Do you know where it leads?"

The pickpocket answered after the fashion of an American "yeggman"—out of the corner of his mouth without the slightest movement of his lips.

"Upstairs," he said.

"What is up there?"

"Chang's private apartments."

"Any smoking?"

"If there is, it is only for those he knows well enough to trust."

"Do you think I could wangle it? Is there any tale you could tell?"

The pickpocket looked about him swiftly.

"Look here, you've got to come across pretty generously if I am to go on with this. I have done all I promised. If Chang found me double-crossing him, my life wouldn't be worth twopence. And I don't want to die yet."

"You can name your own figure. Get me upstairs, where I can have a chance of watching that pair and you can write your own cheque. As for Chang—I can prove a more powerful friend than he can an enemy. I'm going to get him anyway before I finish, so take your choice."

"You'll play on the level with me? You'll stand by me if the Yard is after me?"

"I have already given my word as to that, and I don't break it."

"I know that—every guy who ever speaks of you says you can be trusted. Well, wait by the table and I'll see what I can wangle. I'll have to bluff that you are loaded with money and I want to get you well soaked before I trim you."

Blake nodded and moved back to the table. Under cover of the play he managed to convey to Tinker that no matter what happened he was to stand tight right where he was, then he threw some coins on the cards.

He had seen the pickpocket move away, and, after a few moments, he saw him in conversation with a Chinaman at the upper end of the room. Blake paid them no attention, but out of the corner of his eye he could see that the Chinaman looked his way more than once.

Presently they both walked down the room, until they were near the door through which Chang and Jules had disappeared. The Chinaman opened this and disappeared leaving the crook standing in the corner.

He remained there until the Chink returned about five minutes later and again an earnest conversation took place. After that the crook left the Chink standing and came across to Blake. He touched his arm and motioned for him to follow.

Blake, his eyes as bleary as he could make them, and with a slight lurch to his walk, did so. On reaching the corner, the Chinaman eyed him closely for a full minute. Then abruptly he spoke, using perfect English:

"You wish some other form of amusement?" he asked.

Blake nodded. He then spoke, using English, but with the slur of a Levantine mongrel, such as one would see in Port Said.

"Yes. This game is too slow for me. I am only in England for a short time. My friend here knows what I want. I'll pay well, but I must have it if I can get it."

"You know the risk. I don't say we have anything like that here and I can't talk further, unless you can give me some proof."

Blake smiled, showing discoloured teeth.

"I can give you lots," he said. "Ever hear of Peter O'Halloran in Port Said? He is known to everyone who handles the 'stuff.'"

"I have heard that name," confessed the Chinaman cautiously. "Any others?"

Blake bent closer.

"Ever been in Bombay or Calcutta?"

He took this chance, knowing that Willie Chang was supposed to have had agents in India, when he was peddling opium before his arrest, and because it was whispered that Chang had lain low in Calcutta before slipping back into England.

"I know Bombay and the other place," was the answer.

"Haridas Givingee, of Bombay, knows me well—very well indeed. also I am on intimate terms with Padnam Arrabu, of Calcutta." (Statements which were perfectly true, but not quite in the way which the Chinaman thought.) He recognised the name of Haridas Givingee as Chang's former Bombay agent, and any dope dealer who had ever had any dealing with India would have known the name of Padnam Arrabu—the fat old babu in Calcutta, who was one of the worst crooks from Port Said to Shanghai.

As he finished speaking Blake thrust his hand in an inner pocket and took out a crumpled banknote.

It had been folded, however, so that one could see the denomination at once; and the Chink could make out that the word was "twenty." His eyes shone with sudden greed as Blake slipped it into his hand and as it disappeared from view, he said:

"Wait here. I will see what I can do. But I promise nothing."

He disappeared through the door again and Blake caught sight of what he thought would be there—a flight of stairs. Then the door closed, and he and the crook were alone.

"You are playing a mighty dangerous game," whispered the latter. "If I had known I was in for this I wouldn't have come."

"Don't you worry. I'll see this through. If I go up you stick down here and keep close to the lad. I shan't be long, in any event."

He could say no more then, for the Chinaman came back, and, after shooting a significant glance at the pickpocket, nodded to Blake.

"You come with me," he said. "The boss wants to see you."

Blake turned and followed the Chinaman up the stairs. At the top a single light was burning and they passed down a narrow, gloomy hall, on each side of which were many doors—all closed.

Blake trod lightly, trying his best to listen as he went along, and once, when about half way down, he thought he heard the sudden outburst of a woman's voice. But it passed so swiftly he could not be sure, and he dared not investigate further.

His guide paused before a door at the end of the corridor, and, after knocking, opened it. He stepped in, signing for Blake to follow. The latter did so and found himself facing Chang and Jules.

The room was furnished more like an ordinary office than anything else, and Willie Chang was seated at the roll-top desk like any honest business man. In a chair close to him was Jules, who leant back in a bored way as Chang shot a searching glance at Blake.

"What is it you want?" he asked curtly. "I have already explained. I was given to understand that I might have a smoke here."

"Who told you that?"

"The man who brought me. I forget his name, but he is a friend of a man I met to-day in London. He told me this man could take me wherever I wanted to go. And I want a smoke. My throat is as dry as sand."

"Where do you come from?"

"Port Said and any place out there."

"You say you know Peter O'Halloran, of Port Said. Is that the truth?"

"It is. I can tell you something that will prove it."

"What is that?"

Blake glanced at Jules as if uncertain whether to speak in front of him or not. But Chang signed for him to go on. Then Blake took a step forward and, bending forward, whispered:

"Do you know why Peter O'Halloran went to Syria a few months ago?"

"I—have heard. I came through that way not long ago myself."

"Well, I was mixed up in that deal. If O'Halloran were here, he could tell you so himself."

"What about Bombay and Calcutta?"

"I have already told your man that I know Haridas Givingee, of Bombay, and Padnam Arrabu, of Calcutta."

"If I do as you ask it will cost you money?"

"I expect that—in this country. I have plenty."

"I'll risk it."

With that Willie Chang turned to the Chinaman, who had brought Blake up.

"Give him a room, and what he wants," he ordered curtly. "Before you leave him, he will have to give you fifty pounds in advance. Those are the only terms."

8. In the Opium Den—Blake Feigns Sleep—Proof of His Suspicions—Discovery!

BLAKE was only too pleased to got away without further searching questions on the part of Chang. He followed the other Chinaman through the half-open door and along the corridor to a door on the right.

On the way down the hall Blake had counted the doors on each side, and he knew there were exactly eight, each door opposite the other, making sixteen in all.

It was the fifth door from the end which his guide opened, so Blake knew there were just three more between him and the head of the stairs.

The room was small and, with the exception of a mattress in one corner and a small tabourette, appeared devoid of furniture. There was a single electric light bulb, which was covered with a thick orange shade and, when it was turned on, it did little more than dispel the full darkness.

Blake, who knew the routine of an opium-smoking joint from old experience, squatted down on the mattress and waited. The Chinaman went away, but came back in a few minutes with the complete paraphernalia for smoking.

On the tabourette he placed the "pipe," a little spirit lamp, the needle, and a small tin of treacly-looking brown stuff which Blake knew was prepared opium. He lit the spirit lamp, and then, without a word, held out his hand.

Blake knew what he wanted, so thrusting his hand in his pocket he pulled out a bundle of Treasury notes. He counted off fifty of these and passed them over.

"How long can I stay?" he asked in a low tone.

The Chinaman shrugged.

"As long as you wish—until morning. You will have enough by then?"

"Yes. My friends below—what of them?"

"I will tell them. They can go or stay, as they please."

"All right. I have everything here. Don't let me be disturbed."

"You will be left alone unless you make a noise."

With that the Chinaman left the room, closing the door after him. As soon as he was gone Blake settled down on the mattress, cross-legged, and picked up the needle. He dipped the point of the "yen-hok" in the treacle and gave it a little twist which left a small pill on the end. He took the pipe in his left hand, and then held the "yen-hok" over the flame with his right.

The "cooking" of the opium pill before smoking is a very delicate business, and needs an experienced hand to perform it successfully.

But Blake knew the process as well as any Chinaman, and he twisted and turned, raised and lowered the "yen-hok" as slowly and methodically as if he spent every available hour of his time with the "pipe."

And he had a reason—a very strong reason for doing so. He did not for a moment think that Willie Chang would permit him to go into one of the private rooms for a smoke without making sure that there was no danger to be apprehended from him. He had had his one lesson at the hands of the police, and he would be very very careful that he was not given a second if he could help it.

Therefore, while he had apparently accepted Blake's story and, of course, had felt from the start that he must be all right to be brought to the place by the pickpocket, he would not let it rest there.

And Blake felt that for some time at least he would be subjected to a very careful espionage until it was felt that he was "safe."

For that reason be conducted himself just as any genuine "hophead" would have done. He knew a trick about smoking opium, and he knew that he could bring that into play if he was careful. That trick was simply that he would not inhale the smoke.

The effect of the drug, when smoked, entirely depends on the length of time which it is held in the lungs. It takes from thirty seconds to two minutes and a half to "cook" the pill, depending on how quickly a man works, and in three deep draws it is entirely gone.

If one does not take the smoke past the throat, one can go through a good many pipes without going "hop"; but it takes care to do that.

Blake finished his first pill and placed it over the tiny hole in the middle of the wide, flat bowl of the pipe. He thrust the mouthpiece between his lips and took a deep draw, the while he kept twisting and turning the pill with the "yen-hok." He kept the smoke in the back of his mouth for half a minute or so, then he exhaled it. A second and a third draw he took, and then he flipped the solid ash of the pill off with the "yen-hok."

Phlegmatically he began to prepare a second pill. He worked as slowly and as methodically as before, but all the time his ears were strained to catch the slightest sound. He could hear nothing and, even though he looked all about the room, he could see no spot where a spy might be lurking outside.

But he knew that meant nothing. The Chinese are past masters in the art of espionage, and he knew that there might be a dozen invisible spots from which he could be overlooked.

He smoked the second pipe, and then began on a third. He settled down a little more now, but he was not unwise enough to pretend that he was feeling the effects of the two pills. Only a novice at the game would have done that. He allowed his lids to droop a little more, but that was all.

And it was just as he was on the point of placing the third pill on the bowl that, without the slightest warning, the door flew open.

On the threshold stood the Chinaman who had shown him into the room. He looked at Blake keenly, then he came forward and laid a spare tin of opium on the tabourette.

"This is a gift for you to take away with you," he said. "But you must be careful of it."

Blake nodded, scarcely lifting his heavy lids.

"Very good of you." he responded. "I wanted to ask for one but thought I had better not."

"It is all right. Now I'll leave you."

Again Blake nodded, but saw that the Chinaman had noticed the two little hard ash balls of the first two pipes and, in that moment, he had proof enough that he was treading a dangerous path.

The Chinaman departed again, and Blake went on with his third pipe as usual. He dallied a little after that, but when ten minutes or so had passed, he again dipped the "yen-hok" in the open tin and began to prepare another "pill." He smoked this methodically, then lay back, closing his eyes as if he were beginning to feel the effect of the drug.

He lay absolutely motionless for a long time. He did not know how long he would have to remain thus, but his instinct told him that he would be inspected again. And he was.

It came so softly, so stealthily that he scarcely knew he was not alone until, from beneath the veriest slits, he could see a figure against the wall on the left.

Close to him was a narrow opening through which it had come, and Blake knew that a secret panel had been opened. He could not see the identity of the other, and he dared not open his eyes.

He could see something moving though, and the form approached closer and closer to where he lay. He knew what his fate would be if by any chance he had been betrayed or if he was suspect.

It took all his nerve to lie there, motionless, while that other crept towards him, for it was quite possible that a knife would be seeking his heart if he had been discovered.

Still, he did not move, and he dared not twist his head to try and see what the other did when he reached the tabourette. But he heard a faint tinkle, and he guessed the man was counting the little ash pellets which he had dropped on the tabourette.

There was a little silence, then Blake saw the form moving again, and realised the fellow was half-way back to the secret panel. A few moments later he had stolen out, and the panel slid to as noiselessly as if it ran in a bath of oil.

Still Blake lay supine. Five minutes, ten minutes passed. Then he lifted himself drowsily and turned to the tabourette. He picked up the "yen-hok" lazily, muttering to himself as he did so.

He prepared the pill clumsily, but not so much so that he allowed it to scorch. Then he smoked the fifth pipe and, when he had deposited the ash on the tabourette, set about preparing still another.

But he did not finish this. Instead, he allowed the pipe to fall from his hand, and fell back as if overcome by the fumes. He lay like a log for what he guessed must be a quarter of an hour. He had listened with all his ears during that time, but had heard not a sound.

And now he rose softly to his feet. He might be moving too soon, but that was a risk he had to take, for he knew Tinker would be getting nervous and anxious, and, moreover, it was impossible to tell when something might "break."

He touched the pocket where his automatic lay concealed, and then he stole across to the secret panel. He had a pretty good idea how it would work and now he knew just where to look for it.

He fumbled about for a little until he found the secret which wasn't much after all, for he merely had to locate the almost invisible crack on the right side of the panel.

He slid it back gently and stepped into what he could just see was a narrow passage. He guessed it must have been built along the wall in the room adjoining the one he had just left.

He followed it to the right, and, as he expected, came to another panel a few feet on. This, he figured, must open into the hall by which he had reached the room, and being practically invisible he had not seen it in passing.

He fumbled about there for a little, but to his chagrin found that what he thought would be a movable panel was not one. He was puzzled and stood listening, casting about for some solution.

He turned to the left and began fumbling about there. If he should discover a panel he thought it would lead into the room adjoining his, and that might be occupied. He did find a panel a few seconds later, and, taking the risk of being discovered, slid it back. He found himself gazing into a very narrow passage which had a light at the far end. And now he realised what it meant.

From his room, right along to the end where Willie Chang's private bureau was located a false passage had been built which must feed all the other rooms between the fifth and the last.

In order to enter them one would have to pass through two doors, across this false passage and, since it did not continue the full length of the main corridor, Blake concluded that only Willie Chang's most trusted clients would be allowed to use those rooms. He, being suspected, had been shown into just an ordinary apartment.

He stepped through the opening and began tip-toeing along. As he did so he passed first one closed door, then another and another, and this told him his deductions were correct. He counted a fourth door, and that he knew ought to be the last.

The single light was now just about eight feet ahead of him and immediately beyond a blank wall. If he were travelling, as he thought, then he knew that beyond that blank wall should be Willie Chang's private room.

And as he realised that Chang might come through a panel at any moment he loosened his automatic and dropped it in the outer pocket of his coat where he could whip it out quickly if necessary.

He paused under the light and studied the wall ahead. He thought he could see signs of a panel, so he took another two steps forward until he could reach out his fingers and touch it. He was just on the point of doing so when suddenly he paused for his ear had caught the sound of a voice.

He bent his head until he was almost touching the panel, and now he realised that the division must be only of very thin match-boarding.

He stood scarcely breathing, straining to hear what was being said. And then for a few seconds his pulses hammered heavily against the drums of his ears as he recognised Willie Chang's voice and heard him say:

"—and, anyway, the servant will keep us posted. She says he knows it was Sexton Blake out there with the man from Scotland Yard. He came alone the next morning, but hasn't been there since. We'll have to handle her carefully. She's a fool, but she is scared, and I'll keep her that way. I've had two men out after this bird Blake, and if he gets too busy we'll 'bump' him off."

Then Blake heard a laugh which he guessed came from the throat of the Frenchman. A second later he was sure, for he heard an obviously Latin accent as someone else said:

"That's your job. He is a dangerous man. Don't make a mistake if you do go after him."

"You leave that to me," responded Chang. "And now let's get down to the other business. We haven't any time to lose about settling what is to be done. There is all the money and the other place. Besides, that cargo has got to be shifted. If we are caught with that we might just as well order our coffins at once. And these cursed police are not going to take me a second time."

"Well, then, about the money first, or shall we discuss the cargo? I have everything ready in Paris for the transfer, and the ship will be at La Rochelle in another ten days or so. How many—"

But the Frenchman was not destined to finish that sentence just then, nor were Sexton Blake's ears to pick up the secret for which he was so eagerly straining for, somewhere along the passage, there came the loud banging of a door, and then the rapid patter of feet as someone ran down the passage.

Standing where he was Blake could hear the corridor door of Chang's room thrown open, and then he recognised the voice of the Chinaman who had guided him to his room, as he said swiftly, in Cantonese:

"We have been betrayed, Chang. Lee Won has just telephoned through that Sexton Blake, the detective, left his house in Baker Street to-night disguised as some sort of dark man. With him was his assistant also disguised. They were in the company of 'Slick' Beecher, the pickpocket, and he has just got wind that they came this way. He asked me if they were here, and if they were, to 'get' them quick!"

Blake heard a chair jerked back, but still he stuck where he was.

He wanted to hear what Chang would say. He spoke almost at once, his voice like dripping ice water.

"Sexton Blake—disguised as a dark man —with Slick Beecher—then that is the man who is smoking opium in the room along the corridor."

"It must be," admitted the other Chinaman slowly.

Just then the Frenchman broke in, asking what was the matter, but Chang silenced him. He continued speaking in Cantonese to his man.

"Go and see," he ordered. "He is still there. He was asleep or feigning to be asleep when I looked in. Kill him, and do it quick. Kill the man Blake, and then 'get' the other two in the gambling-room. I shall go there also. Don't kill Slick Beecher unless it is necessary. I want him for myself. I'll handle him first for this betrayal. Now go!"

And as Blake heard the sound of the other Chinaman's feet pattering softly along the corridor he sped back along the secret passage to the room where he was supposed to be lying.

9.   A Life and Death Struggle to Escape from Willie Chang's Hands—Information for Scotland Yard.

BLAKE did not attempt to reach the mattress in the corner of the room. He knew that it would be a race between him and the Chinaman to reach the room itself—the Chink along the pucca corridor and himself along the false passage.

He did pause to close the secret panel, however, then he whirled round the short turn and through the other panel into the room he had left.

He had no time to close the second panel, for even as he went through the opening, he saw the door of the room begin to swing open.

It was not flung wide as before. This time, the Chinaman who had been ordered to kill him, was acting cautiously, and it was just that which gave Blake time to cover the distance from the panel to the door. He did not draw his weapon, for he wanted to do what had to be done with a minimum of noise.

He kept behind the door until it was nearly half open; then, as he knew from that angle, the Chink would be able to see that the mattress was unoccupied, he sprang. He swung round the edge of the door to find the celestial in a half-crouch, a long-bladed knife in his hand.

He was startled at Blake's sudden appearance, for, whatever he may have discovered since his last visit to the room, he had firmly believed that Blake was genuinely smoking the drug.

Blake took full advantage of his momentary hesitancy. Before the other could recover and bring the knife down Blake was in under his guard. The Chinaman came to life swiftly, and his mouth opened to give a yell of warning to Willie Chang; but the white man's hands were at his throat, and with a terrific heave Blake dragged him inside the room.

With his heel he kicked the door until it almost closed; then, as the Chink twisted like an eel in his grasp, trying to force the point of the knife into his body Blake jerked one hand away, and, catching the other's right wrist, flung his whole weight into the pressure.

The man could not resist the awful pain of those twisting bones. No human being could have withstood the agony of it. Despite himself he was forced to yield, and slowly, ever so slowly, Blake got the arm down and around to the back until he could jam it high up between the fellow's shoulder blades—one of the most painful ju-jitsu attacks known.

The knife fell with a clatter to the floor. The Chinaman was gasping like a half-spent fish, trying with every shred of will power to force his vocal chords to obey him. He was trying to yell, to scream, to send out a crashing warning to Chang. But nothing but short agonised gasps hissed between his teeth.

Sexton Blake knew that the voice would come soon though, and he was determined that he should choke it off before it could emerge into full volume. Therefore he wasted no time. He jammed the twisted arm up still higher until it seemed to have reached the very limit of the ball and socket control; then he stiffened, and gave one sharp, sudden push, the weight of his uprising body behind the pressure.

The terrific pain loosed the choking that had held the Chinaman's voice in check, and a scream was just on the point of being born when Blake's hands once more caught him by the flesh of the throat, strangling the cry off into a tortured sob.

He held the celestial with his left hand and loosed his right. He, drew it back, the fist clenched. Then he drove it forward, a terrific short jab to the point of the chin, and, as the knuckle hit the point with wicked impact, he let go with his left hand. The Chinaman went down in a clean knockout, and Blake stepped back panting.

He took one look at the unconscious Chink. He knew pretty well what was behind that last blow, and he figured the other would remain as he was for a good twenty minutes at least. Blake was no "orchid fighter," and when he hit for a knock-out he usually managed to gauge it as he wanted it.

He stole to the door and listened. He thought he heard a sound along the corridor, and guessed that Chang was coming. He remembered that the Chinaman had said that he would go to the gambling-room, and he had probably delayed just long enough to tell the Frenchman what had happened, and also to give his henchman time to finish off Blake.

Blake knew that, if he were to get clear, he would have to reach the gambling-room first. So there was no time now for finesse. If Chang were coming, then he would have to tackle him and the Frenchman in the corridor. He pulled out his automatic and stepped into the hall. Just as he did so he caught sight of a figure in the very act of emerging from Chang's room.

He turned to the right, and raced for the head of the stairs. He had gone less than half a dozen feet when he heard a startled curse at the other end of the hall, then a pistol crashed out.

A bullet whistled past Blake's ear, and he ducked against the wall. He gave a quick zig-zag to the left, another to the right, and then he held the centre of the corridor as the pistol crashed out a second time, and a bullet crashed into the wall close to where he had been a second before. He heard someone cry out, and the sound of opening doors.

Willie Chang called out a harsh order to someone, and then, as he gave vent to a string of vile curses, he shot again. That time the bullet ripped through the shoulder of Blake's coat, but still he did not turn.

He was just a few feet from the head of the staircase now, and he covered the remaining distance in a couple of leaps.

He dashed down half a dozen steps, and there he paused. He turned, finding that he could just see over the top step and along the hall. Willie Chang was coming towards him on the run, a pistol held ready for use. And even as Blake ducked instinctively the weapon roared out.

Blake clawed his own automatic, and sent a "snap" shot in the direction of the flying figure. He deliberately shot low, but missed, for although Chang drew up, he did not falter.

There was another figure behind him, and, as a yell of pain broke out, Blake saw that it was the Frenchman, Jules. He stumbled against the wall, and several heads that had been thrust out into the corridor suddenly disappeared.

Chang shot again, but Blake already ducked, and before the Chinaman could pull again, Blake had bobbed up at one side of the stairs. He fired low again, then, as he saw Chang start to retreat, he turned and sped swiftly down the remaining stairs.

He reached the door at the bottom, and flung it open. Instantly he saw that serious trouble was afoot.

No definite attack had been made upon Tinker and Slick Beecher, but Blake noticed that the greater proportion of Chinamen in the room had gathered in the vicinity, and were slowly but surely pressing Tinker and the pickpocket away from the upper end towards one of the lower corners.

He knew that Willie Chang and the Frenchman would be down the stairs in a few seconds. He knew, too, that the sound of shots above must have been heard, for, as he plunged through the doorway, a score of yellow faces turned his way.

There was only one chance, and that was to strike before Chang came on the scene, and before the celestials knew just what they should do.

He flung the door closed, and looked to see if there was a key. There was not even a latch, and he had no time to sling a barricade in front of it. He thought he heard a clatter of feet on the stairs, so, bringing his heavy automatic up from behind his leg where it had been concealed, he dashed forward towards the spot where Tinker and Beecher were standing.

It was just then that Tinker spotted him, and, on seeing the weapon in Blake's hand, he drew his own.

The action was as if a signal had been given to the Chinks, for almost with one accord those who were surrounding him produced knives, and advanced in a threatening manner. At the same moment the staircase door was flung open, and Blake heard Willie Chang's high-pitched voice yelling out a stream of Cantonese.

Blake fired one shot high, then he plunged forward, driving his way through the press as if he were in a football scrum. He waved his arm towards the door, and yelled to Tinker to make in that direction.

Beecher was as white as a sheet, but now that the crisis was upon him, he was game enough. He had jerked out a small nickle-plated revolver, and was watching Blake. He saw Blake's gesture, and turned with Tinker.

Tinker shot once, high as he had seen Blake aim, then he drove ahead, trying to reach the point where his path would converge with Blake's.

But Willie Chang's voice had roused the celestials into full action. Half a dozen sprang forward, trying to overwhelm Tinker and Beecher, while a full dozen or more swung and made for Blake.

Blake did not attempt to shoot high a second time. There was red murder in those oblique eyes that he faced, and he knew if they were to get out of the place alive it would be only in one way. It was their lives against those of the yellow mongrels, and he did not hesitate.

The heavy automatic spat out as he shot low.

Bang! Bang! Bang!

Three times he, fired, and each time a yellow fiend went down with a yell. Across the mob Tinker had followed suit, and of the half dozen who had rushed him and Beecher, three went down while the others paused. Tinker whirled, and literally lifted Beecher along with him.

Blake kept on travelling, and clubbed a way through to the spot which was his objective without shooting again. But just then Willie Chang began shooting from the other end of the room. He was screaming like a maniac, and Blake caught enough to know that Chang was threatening all sorts of dire things to his henchmen if they allowed him to escape alive.

The voice of the dope peddler spurred them on again, and this time they came on in a determined rush just as Tinker and Beecher reached Blake's side.

"No use holding!" yelled Blake above the uproar. "Shoot fast, and make every shot tell! Get busy with that toy, Beecher!"

The words were accompanied by a crashing roar of the big automatic, and so quickly did Tinker follow suit, that the two explosions sounded almost together.

Then Blake shot again, and following that sounded the thinner bark of the pickpocket's weapon as he got into action. They backed slowly towards the door, but Chang saw their manoeuvre, and came pelting through his men, frothing with rage and utterly reckless of consequences.

Blake swung the automatic round and shot. If that bullet had found its mark one of the vilest creatures living would have passed out for ever. But even as Blake's finger flexed on the trigger a Chink stumbled across in front of Chang and took the bullet to his side.

From one side came a knife, flying viciously through the air. It passed between Blake and Tinker, but they heard a startled yelp of pain as it plunged into Beecher's shoulder.

Blake held his fire then, for he knew his clip was getting low. He took one quick look behind him, and saw the door not three feet away. He saw, too, that Beecher was out of the fight, although he was still on his feet. He turned to Tinker.

"Shoot Chang if he comes on," he ordered. "Keep the others off at any cost! I'll see to the door."

He sprang back and tried the handle. As he expected, it was locked. He placed the barrel of the automatic against it and pulled the trigger. Then, lifting his foot, he drove it hard against the panels. The door crashed open, and, turning, Blake took one more shot at the mob. Then he shot out an arm and swept Tinker and Beecher through the opening.

"Now for it!" he panted. "Out the way we came in! I'll hold them back while you get the street door open."

Tinker and Beecher raced on, while Blake whirled round. Chang had gone completely off his head. He was raving like a madman, and came plunging on towards the door, shooting wildly as he came.

Blake waited for a second or so, then he shot again. But for the second time Fate fooled him. Just as before a celestial fell in front of Chang, and the bullet plunged into his body. It was as if the dope peddler bore a charmed life. And as he still kept on, the mob at his heels, Blake took one more pot shot and fled.

He raced through the empty room by way of which they had come, and then out into the hall. He saw that Tinker and Beecher had managed to get the front door open, so he kept going.

They plunged through, with Blake after them, and stumbled to the street. Blake took time enough to slam the door, then all three tore up the street, Blake and Tinker helping Beecher, who was obviously in great pain, and was getting weak from loss of blood.

Blake's chief hope was that the taxi-man had been so well satisfied with his tip that he would hang about as he had intimated, and they had just swung the corner when he caught sight of a cab.

They reached it, and one glance told Blake that it was the same. He jerked open the door, and bundled Tinker and Beecher into it. The man must have been on the alert, for he was already starting his engine, and as he swung to the seat Blake cried:

"Up west—any place—and drive like mad!"

He jumped on to the running-board, and the taxi started with a jerk just as the first of the Chinese swung round the corner. Blake fired his last shot into them, then he swung inside and closed the door. The driver needed no urging with that murderous crew in pursuit, and drove as if his life depended on it—which it did.

They turned corner after corner, taking them almost on two wheels, until they banged into the Commercial Road. There the man slowed down somewhat, for it was hardly likely the mob would follow that far.

Not until they reached the Strand did Blake put his head out and gave him the Baker Street address. They reached home safely, but, as Blake started to get out, he found that Beecher had suddenly slumped back. One look at the pickpocket was enough to tell him what had happened.

"He's gone, Tinker," he said— "fainted from loss of blood. We'll have to carry him in, and get Dr. Fraser as quickly as possible."

They got him out between them, and carried him up the steps. Blake told the taximan to wait, and by this time the latter was beginning to guess that his strange fare was something very different from what he appeared.

They got Beecher on to the couch in the consulting-room, and then, while Blake went out to pay off the man and tell him enough to ensure that he would not talk about the events of the evening, the lad rang up Dr. Fraser, the physician whom Blake usually employed.

A quarter of an hour later Beecher had been put to bed in one of the spare rooms, and a nurse had been sent for. It was a nasty wound in the shoulder, and would keep Beecher incapacitated for some few weeks to come. But the doctor assured Blake that it was not necessarily dangerous, the chief anxiety being due to the quantity of blood which the man had lost.

When Dr. Fraser had taken his departure, Blake sat down at his desk and drew the telephone instrument towards him. Lifting the receiver, he got through to Scotland Yard, but found that Inspector Thomas was not on duty.

He had hardly hoped to find him there at that hour of the morning (it was now getting on for three o'clock), unless he should be engaged on some important case, so he hung up the receiver, and, after a few moments wait, gave the number of the inspector's private house in Maida Vale.

A voice answered after some delay, and when he recognised it as that of Inspector Thomas, Blake apologised for disturbing him at that hour.

"I shouldn't have done so," he went on, "only I have just secured some important information which I think you will be anxious to have."

"That's all right, Blake," said Thomas, still drowsily. "What is the information?"

"Willie Chang is back in England!"

"What?" All sleepiness was now gone from the inspector's tones, and Blake smiled.

"It is a fact," he added. "Willie Chang is back in England. I have seen him tonight, and have positive proof that he is back in the old game of dope peddling. If you want to gather him in, I can tell you where he is hanging out—or was up to half an hour ago."

"Of course I want to rope him in! I hadn't an idea he had sneaked back. I thought he got a sufficient dose the last time. Where can we find him?"

"He is running a gambling and dope joint in Cairo Street, Limehouse. It is a cul-de-sac, and it is the last house on the left. There is a big crowd of Chinks in the place, so you will need a good-sized force for the raid."

"I'll 'phone the Yard at once, and go on inside an hour. How did you discover this?"

"It is too long a story now. I'll tell you later on. But that is not all, inspector. With Willie Chang is a Frenchman. His name is Jules. He is a small man physically, clean-shaven except for a small black moustache. His hair is artificially crimped or waved, his face typically French in form and colouring, and his hands particularly noticeable for their whiteness. He is a hairdresser by profession. I have very urgent reason for wanting him roped in as well. Will you try and get him?"

"You bet your sweet life I will! What is the charge?"

"I'll only say now that it may develop into one of murder. I shall come on to the Yard after the round up, and go into everything with you. But I think every port and air port should be notified without delay, for I have reason to believe that he may try to get out of the country if Chang's place is raided."

"I'll snaffle him if he is there! Is that all?"

"Yes, except to warn you that Chang will expect a raid. There is a canal at the back of the premises, and he may try to escape that way. I would suggest that you throw out a line of your men there to stop that gap."

"You leave that to me! If that bird is there, he won't escape! And I'll broadcast a warning to all ports and air ports. Much obliged for this information, Blake, but I'd like to know what it means."

Blake laughed.

"That is enough to go on with," he said. "I'll be at the Yard as soon as you tell me you have caught the birds, and will explain things then."

With that he hung up, and, turning to Tinker, began to fill his pipe.

"Better turn in, young 'un," he said. "It is late, and we have a good deal to do tomorrow—or, rather, to-day. Was Beecher asleep when you left him?"

"Yes, guv'nor. What are you going to do about him?"

"Keep him here until he is able to leave. We got him into this mess, and we shall have to see him through it. Besides, if he goes abroad at present, either Willie Chang or some of his gang will get him, sure."

"Do you think they will pick up Chang in the raid?"

"I can't tell, but I should say it was about even money betting, the odds depending on how soon the inspector gets his machine into action. Now, clear off, Tinker! I have a lot of thinking to do before I turn in."

10.   Some Strange Facts of the Case—The Funeral Arrangements and Sexton Blake's Mystifying Request.

IT was nearly five o'clock before Sexton Blake left his consulting-room and went along to bed. Ever since Tinker had departed Blake had been seated at his desk smoking pipe after pipe, sometimes staring into space for a quarter of an hour at a time and, again, making odd and seemingly meaningless pencil patterns on a block of paper.

He was not displaying any extraordinary and clairvoyant gifts, such as the novel writers like to endow their detectives with. He was simply bringing to bear, on a very difficult problem, all the power of that finely trained mind which, through long practice, could probe into a mass of confusing events as swiftly and as deftly as the knife of a surgeon.

He was no magician, was Sexton Blake; but he was a very able criminologist, probably the most able in his profession. And in this strange murder case which he was trying to solve he realised that there were many factors connected with it which he had not yet even touched on.

Laid out in sequence the different items seemed to have little relation, one to the other. Everything, in so far as the problem began, started with the puzzling and seemingly motiveless murder of Mrs. McMinn. He had probed into her past as deeply as it was possible, and he was satisfied that McMinn had told him the truth.

There was a woman, on the face of it just an ordinary suburban housewife who for the most part of her life had lived a quiet and uneventful life. As a girl she had resided at Ealing with her parents where, as youngsters, she and John McMinn had been lovers.

Their engagement had followed as an ordinary sequence to courtship, and then had come the only period in her whole life which was not in keeping with the routine which she had known as a girl, and, which she had continued as a married woman.

That one period of time had, according to McMinn, extended over something like a year. An aunt had left her a fair-sized legacy and her parents, just as other parents would have done, had encouraged her to put in a year abroad where she would acquire a "polish" which she could not get at Ealing.

At least, that is what fond parents think when they send their children to Brussels and Paris, but it is entirely a matter of temperament whether such a sojourn does them good or harm.

At any rate, Mrs. McMinn had put in her year in Paris, and on her return had continued her engagement to John McMinn. Perhaps her parents had hoped that she would have met someone a little superior socially, to the young printer, particularly as it seemed that, about that time, his father had failed in the little printing business which he had built up. But evidently no real opposition had been offered, and the marriage had taken place in due course.

After that, or soon after, they had moved to Finsbury Park where for some fifteen years they had lived a quiet and uneventful life, the wife taking a placid interest in the harmless social and church events of the neighbourhood, while the husband had pursued his trade as a steady going citizen.

Then within the space of a few minutes everything was altered. The woman was shot down in cold blood. McMinn was an affectionate husband with no real motive for committing the crime. No weapon had been found, and no one knew of a single soul who could have any possible motive for perpetrating the deed.

And yet—and yet here was a woman like that who had such an inordinant secret vanity that she wore wigs which were made by the master wigmaker of Europe—by the most exclusive hairdresser in Paris, the haunt of the wealthy.

That little green silk cross in each wig had told Sexton Blake where they came from, and he knew that each wig could not have been bought from Jules, the maker, for less than ten thousand francs.

Where had that trail led him? Within a few hours of his arrival in Paris what had he discovered? He had proved that he was correct in assuming that the wigs had been made by the exclusive Jules. But he had found more—found something which, instead of helping him to clear up the mystery, had but deepened it. The wigs were made by Jules, but on the hairdresser's books there was no client of the name of Madame McMinn.

What was her full name? The husband had said it was Bertha McMinn. And the hairdresser in the Champs Elysees in Paris had been making wigs for some years past for a certain mysterious client in England, who was known on the books simply as Madame Berthe, and who sent a special messenger across to France to receive and take back the wigs when required—apparently this occurring about once in every two years.

That in itself was one of the strangest phases of the whole affair. The name Berthe was simply the French rendering of the name Bertha, and the latter was Mrs. McMinn's first name.

But how came it that this quiet-living woman of a London suburb, should go to such pains to secure her wigs at such expense and secrecy? That is if the Madame Berthe of Jules was the woman who had been killed in the villa. And if not then where, when, and how did Mrs. McMinn secure those wigs which Blake had found at the villa?

Then again—shortly after his arrival in Paris, Jules had received a telegram which had caused him to become greatly agitated. He had at once cancelled all his appointments and had left hurriedly for England. Blake had dogged him and had had him followed to a mysterious house in Church Street, in Chelsea.

Investigation of that circumstance, through one of his agents, had revealed the fact that there was a close connection between the house in Chelsea and a joint being run by one Willie Chang, in Limehouse—Willie Chang, a notorious dope peddler, who had been in prison in England, and had then been deported.

Then Blake had visited the joint and found that Jules, the hairdresser of the Champs Elysees was on the most intimate terms with the Chinaman. More than that, he had succeeded in overhearing certain scraps of conversation between the two which had seemed in some way to refer to the murder at the villa.

But why, why, why? In what way could there be a connection? What possible link could there be between Jules and Willie Chang; between Willie Chang and Mrs. John McMinn; between Jules and the same woman? The more he thought of it, the more bewildering did the whole thing seem —utterly fantastic and impossible. And yet— and yet—

Blake was up again at seven. He had just finished his tea and was going into his bath when Tinker came in, fully dressed.

"Inspector Thomas has just called up," he announced.

"What about?"

"The raid on Willie Chang's."

"What happened?"

"Nothing, guv'nor. The whole thing was a wash-out."

"What do you mean?"

"When they got there the place was empty. The inspector wanted to speak with you, but I told him you were sleeping. So he told me what happened."

"Well, get on with the details," said Blake irritably, reaching for a cigarette.

"Just as I said—the place was empty. The birds had flown the coop—skidoo, vanished—just like that."

"Did he find nothing at all?"

"Yes, sir. He says he found enough to prove that you were right about it being a gambling joint and a dope house as well. He also found stains near the door in the big room that looked like blood. But that was all."

"The stains would be from Beecher's wound. It was just what I warned him about—Chang and his gang must have made a getaway by the canal. They must have packed up as soon as we got away."

"It looks that way. At any rate, the inspector is jolly sore, I can tell you. He says he had forty men down there on the raid. He wants to know if you have anything to tell him."

"I should have had if he had nabbed his men. But now—not yet, not yet. By the way, have you seen Beecher this morning? And what about the nurse?"

"She turned up just before I went to bed. Didn't you hear the bell!"

"I wasn't paying any attention. What about Beecher?"

"He is weak, and his wound is bothering him a good deal, but he is quite conscious. He is scared stiff, though, that he will have to leave here. Chang has certainly put the breeze up him."

"He can stay here until he is better. I'll see him before I go out. I am going into my bath now, and I want you to telephone through to Inspector Brown, at Finsbury Park. I think you said the funeral of the woman at the villa would take place today."

"That's what they told me, guv'nor, at the inquest."

"Well, find out the exact time. I want to go out there. And, if the inspector rings up again, tell him I shall call at the Yard or telephone him later in the day. Did he say if he had broadcasted a warning to all ports and air ports?"

"Oh, yes, sir. I forgot to tell you that."

Blake gave a grunt and disappeared, while Tinker went off on his errand. As soon as breakfast was over Blake went along to the spare room to see Beecher. He found a very efficient nurse in charge and, after a few words with her, he sat down beside the pickpocket.

The man was a little feverish, but seemed to be doing as well as could be expected, for he had certainly lost a lot of blood. Blake smiled at him cheerfully.

"You will be quite all right in a few days," he said. "And I want to tell you that you won't have to leave here until it is perfectly safe for you to do so. Chang is on the run now, but we shall nab him before long."

"He's a bad customer, Mr. Blake. He said be would get me, and he will if he can. Even if he has to come here."

"He won't get you. I promise you that. The place was raided during the night, and Chang and his whole gang have gone to earth. Scotland Yard has the case in hand, and they are spreading a net all over the East End. Chang will drop into it before very long and, when he does, he won't get away so easily as he did last time. There is a lot more against him, and he will go up for at least seven years—perhaps a good deal longer if a certain other affair is brought home to him. So you take things easy and don't worry. I am extremely obliged to you for what you did last night, and I shall see that you do not suffer by it. The doctor will be here during the morning and, whatever he says you may have, I shall order."

Beecher seemed easier in his mind after Blake's words, and a few minutes later the detective took his departure. Back in the consulting-room he read the notes Tinker had jotted down.

He found that the funeral was to be at a quarter-past two so, after a few moments thought, he told the lad that he would leave Baker Street at half-past one.

Then they settled down to routine work and, with the exception of two interruptions, were able to continue until Mrs. Bardell served an early lunch.

The first interruption was when Dr. Fraser arrived to pay a visit to Beecher; and the second when Inspector Thomas telephoned through.

Thomas repeated practically what he had said to Tinker, but Blake was no more communicative. In fact, he could not have been so had he wished, for he had little if anything to tell the inspector just then.

When they had finished discussing the raid the inspector asked if Blake would go along with him to the funeral. But Blake declined.

"I'm sorry," he said, "but I don't think you will see me there."

So, somewhat grumpily, the inspector hung up the receiver. Blake lunched lightly, and a few minutes past one sent Tinker round for the Grey Panther. While he was waiting he called up the inspector at Finsbury Park and, after giving his name, asked what local undertaker was attending to the funeral arrangements.

He noted down the name, and when he had rung off looked up the address in the telephone book.

He then went along to his dressing-room, where he tossed a few small objects into a small attache case and, by the time he was back in the consulting-room, Tinker was at the kerb with the car.

Blake's instructions were brief.

"You will remain at home during the afternoon, my lad," he said, before taking the wheel. "I may be back early—or late. I can't tell yet. But I don't want Beecher left alone. You have plenty of work to carry on with, anyway."

"I wish I knew what you were up to," mumbled the lad in a disappointed tone. "I want to be in on the finish of this thing."

"And you will. What I aim to do this afternoon is purely routine work which you can't handle. I wish you could. I should prefer to attend to another phase of the case. But you will see plenty of action yet, or I miss my guess. Now get that frown off your brow and settle down to work."

And Tinker, being a good sportsman, grinned cheerfully.

Blake drove through at a steady pace to Finsbury Park. But he did not proceed direct to Manor House Corner. Instead, he stopped at a certain firm of undertakers in the Seven Sisters Road and, leaving the Grey Panther at the kerb, entered the shop.

He saw several men, dressed in sombre black, grouped about the front shop, and asked one of them if the proprietor was about. He was informed that the gentleman in question was in the back yard, his informant offering to show him through there, if he wished.

Blake indicated that he would be obliged, so they passed through a back workshop, where he saw coffins in all states of manufacture, and into a cobbled yard, where a hearse was standing.

A couple of ostlers were at that moment in the act of backing a pair of black horses, black harnessed and black plumed. Near them stood another man in sombre mourning clothes, and it was to this individual his guide led him.

Blake did not announce his name in front of the other, but asked if he might have an urgent word in private.

The undertaker, impressed by Blake's appearance and manner, readily consented. He led the way back through the workroom and through a door on the left to his private office. As soon as the door was closed Blake took out a card and presented it.

"My name is Blake," he said quietly— "Sexton Blake. I have a favour to ask you, Mr. Daley, and I may say that I am willing to pay whatever fee you wish for the privilege I am going to ask."

"Sexton Blake! You mean you are the famous detective?"

"I am afraid I have been so described at times," returned Blake, with a smile.

"What is it I can do for you, Mr. Blake?" asked the undertaker, obviously considerably impressed by his distinguished visitor. "I shall be only too pleased to oblige you in any way I can."

"It is just this, Mr. Daley. Am I right in assuming that the hearse in the back yard is being harnessed to proceed to the funeral of the late Mrs. McMinn, of Woodberry Down?"

"Quite correct, sir."

"And the men in your front shop are the pallbearers?"

"Yes, sir."

"It is the custom, I believe, to send an extra man to gather together the various items of funeral paraphernalia as soon as the funeral leaves the house?"

"Usually, yes, but not always."

"Was it your intention to do so to-day?"

"Well, as a matter of fact, one of the pallbearers was to go back to the house after the funeral. I have two funerals on this afternoon, and am a little short-handed."

"Ah! Then I shall explain what my request is, Mr. Daley. I have a reason—a perfectly legitimate one, I can assure you —for wanting to take the place of the man you would send to do the collecting of the paraphernalia after the funeral leaves the house. I am sorry that I cannot explain more fully, but I presume it is known to you that the police have strong suspicions that Mrs. McMinn's death was due to foul play. I have a professional interest in the matter, and there is a strong reason why I wish to enter the house this afternoon without my identity being suspected. I am taking you into my confidence, and I know you will respect it."

"Of course. Mr. Blake, of course. Let me think. Why, I think it could be arranged. What about clothes? And then, wouldn't they recognise you? I mean the police?"

"I have come prepared for that," answered Blake. "I have a small attache case in my car which contains certain articles of disguise. If you can supply me with one of your regular black suits I could manage quite well."

"I can do that, and shall be glad to oblige you, sir."

"Thank you, Mr. Daley. If you will please fix on a fee, I shall be most happy to pay it."

"No, sir; not to be thought of. I have followed your cases for years, Mr. Blake, and I consider it a great honour to have a hand in one of them. But you will have to make haste, sir, for the hearse will leave in a few minutes. I take it you want to go on to the house with the others?"

"I should prefer that. I shall get my attache-case at once. I suppose my car will be all right at the kerb?"

"Better drive it round the corner into the back-yard, sir. It will be safer there."

A quarter of an hour later the hearse rolled out of the yard, followed by two carriages containing the pall-bearers. The coach for the solitary mourner was to be sent from a nearby stable.

On the seat beside the driver of the hearse was a black-bearded man, clad, like the others, in sombre black; and even the undertaker had found it difficult to believe that this individual was the well-groomed detective who had been in his office a short time before. He had kept quiet about the whole thing, and not one of the pall-bearers nor the driver of the hearse suspected for a single moment that the extra hand accompanying them was the famous Baker Street criminologist, Sexton Blake.

Blake entered the house with the others; the coffin had been placed in the drawing-room, from which most of the gimcrack, "gilt and gingerbread" furniture had had to be removed.

A solitary relation had put in an appearance to accompany the sorrowing husband to the cemetery, and once the hearse was on the scene, it did not take long to get things started.

It seemed scarcely ten minutes before the little cortege was on its way, and, from behind the blind of the parlour window, Blake saw that both Inspector Thomas and the local inspector were following in a car.

11.   Sexton Blake Puts His Theory to the Test—The Veil of Mystery is Lifted—Blake Shows a Firm Hand.

BLAKE was just turning away from the window when Maggie Williams, the servant, entered the parlour. She stood looking about the disordered room for a few moments, then she addressed the "undertaker's man."

"Are you going to pack up these things?" Blake nodded.

"Yes, my dear," he answered pleasantly. "That is what Mr. Daley sent me here for."

"Well, I'll help you; but not so much of the 'my dear.'"

Blake laughed and set to work, the girl helping him to fold up the various pieces of funeral cloth which were lying about. But all the time Blake was thinking: "Now why is she so anxious to help me? It looks as if she were anxious for me to be gone as soon as possible. If so, what is the reason?"

Between them it did not take long, and Blake was casting about in his mind for some excuse to remain in the house, when there came the sharp whir of a bell somewhere at the back.

Out of the corner of his eye Blake saw the girl glance at him sharply and then half turn towards the door as if undecided. Blake tossed a piece of black velvet on top of the pile he had made, and then straightened up as if he had not heard the bell.

"That will do for now, I think," he said. "I am much obliged to you, my dear. I shall go back now, but when the cart calls for these you might deliver them to the man."

"All right," she replied in a tone of slight impatience. "You say you are going back now?"

Blake reached for his hat.

"There isn't anything more to be done here. I shall— But isn't that a bell ringing somewhere?"

"Yes—the back door. It is only one of the tradesmen."

"Well, run along and answer it, my dear. I can let myself out."

With that he opened the door into the hall and walked along towards the front door. As he laid his fingers on the handle he half turned and saw that the girl was standing at the lower end of the hall, watching him.

"Good-bye," he called, with a smile. "And thank you for your help."

He turned the handle and opened the door, taking good care,

nevertheless, to keep an eye on the girl as he did so. Just then the back-door bell went for the third time, and as he started through the front doorway, Blake saw the girl disappear from view.

He took a step out on to the small porch; then he turned as if to close the door after him. He could see right along to the back of the front hall, but the girl was not in sight, so, swiftly and silently, he stepped back into the hall. Then he slammed the door heavily, so that it could be heard in every part of the house.

He sped on tiptoe down the hall until he reached the door of the sitting-room on the right. He pushed open the door there and stepped inside.

He was taking an awful chance, but so far, he thought, he was safe, and it was not unlikely that the girl would think he had slammed the door when he passed out. If she did not run through to see if he was really gone, he had a slim chance of pulling the trick off.

He half closed the door of the sitting-room and cast about for some place to conceal himself.

There was a couch in one corner, but it did not offer sufficient cover, and all he could see that held any promise were two heavy serge curtains that hung over the window, one on each side.

He tiptoed across the room and got behind one just as he heard a door close, and then the sound of voices in the hall outside. He strained forward to listen, and his lids narrowed a little as he heard the accents of Jules, the French hairdresser.

"Are you sure?" he was demanding, apparently of the girl.

"Yes, he has just gone. I saw him go out the door. You must have heard it slam."

"I heard it—yes; but we shall look about."

Footsteps followed, and Blake could picture the Frenchman and the maid looking in the parlour. A few seconds later he heard a sound at the door of the sitting-room, and then came the girl's voice:

"I tell you he is gone. You have seen the other rooms, and he is not upstairs."

"I think you are right, mademoiselle. And now for the key. Have you found it?"

"I don't know who you are. I am frightened of all this. Why didn't he come?"

"Now, no nonsense!" was the sharp reply. "I explained at the door that he dared not come. It was safer for me to come. And you will be a lot more afraid if you don't do as you are told. Have you found the key which he telephoned to you about? If so, hand it over, for I must get away quickly."

"I—I found it; but all this makes me afraid. When I did what he asked I never knew such a terrible thing would happen. The police keep asking me questions all the time, and that man Sexton Blake was here."

"So he told me. Has he been back?"

"No. But he may return; and if he does, I am sure he will find out something. He sees everything, and they say he never fails."

"Poof! That is silly talk. He failed in what he tried to do last night. Come now, the key, and then I will tell you what he says you must do."

There was a slight pause, and then Blake heard Jules voice again. It was exultant.

"That is it—that is it! You have done well. Where did you find it?"

"Under the mattress of her bed."

"Just where I thought. That is a French trick, that. Here is the ten pounds which he promised you if you found it. And now, before I get back, I shall tell you what you must do. You have got to leave here."

"Leave here. What do you mean? I can't do that. If I run away, they will think I did—that."

"You are in greater danger if you stay. The police are getting hold of some clues, and, sooner or later, they will arrest you on suspicion. Then, when they question you, 'he' is afraid that you will break down and tell more than you ought. So you must leave and it must be to-night. You have nothing to fear. We shall keep you in a safe hiding place until the thing is all over and you will be well paid."

"I—can't—I can't. Oh, I am afraid. Why did I ever—"

"Shut up."

The man spat the words out viciously as the girl began to get hysterical and she grew silent. Then Blake could hear him hiss, as venomously as a snake:

"You know what happened to 'her'? Do you want the same thing to happen to you? If you don't do just as you are told—if you play us false—if you do not come to-night to the place of which I shall tell you, then that thing will happen to you. Do you understand?"

Only a low moan answered him.

"Do you understand?"

"Oh, yes. What am I to do?"

"Here is a piece of paper on which I have written the address. This evening you will ask your master to allow you to go out for a walk. After what has taken place here to-day he will not refuse. Do not attempt to take any bag with you. Put what trinkets you want in your pockets and that is all. Everything else will be provided for you. As soon as you are clear of the house, go to the Underground station and take a train to Liverpool Street.

"At Liverpool Street you will take a No. 11 bus, which will drop you at the corner of the street the name of which is on this piece of paper. Then walk along to the address which is there and ring the bell at exactly ten o'clock. You will be admitted at once, and then you will be safe—quite safe. Do you understand?"

"Y-yes."

"And you will not fail?"

"N-no."

"That is well. And, remember, if you do fail you will be dead before to-morrow morning. Now let me out."

They moved away, then, and a few moments later Blake heard a door close. He stood just where he was, giving the Frenchman time to get down the garden and along the river path to the bridge, for he had already figured he had come that way.

At the end of a couple of minutes or so, he stepped out from behind the curtain and walked lightly across to the door. He stood just inside, waiting and listening.

Presently he heard a door open and the sound of a slow footstep coming along. Then he could hear someone sobbing—a woman. Still he stood waiting, until the footsteps were just outside the sitting-room door.

And then, jerking the door open, he was out into the hall and had one hand on the woman's shoulder and another over her mouth before she had the slightest warning that he was coming.

He whirled her round and pushed her into the sitting-room. He then forced her into a chair and, bending over her, said harshly:

"Not a sound out of you. Do you understand?"

She nodded mutely and he drew his hand away from her lips. With a quick motion, he jerked off the false beard and moustache and bent over her again.

"Look at me!" he ordered.

She raised frightened eyes to his and as she saw that it was Sexton Blake, the man who had already stricken her with terror, she opened her mouth to scream. But Blake was expecting that and slammed his hand over her lips again.

"Keep quiet!" he snapped, "and you won't be hurt. If you don't you will find yourself in a police cell this night."

He drew his hand away and the girl sat quiet, trembling with fright. Blake still kept his hand on her shoulder and, standing thus, pointed towards the window.

"I was behind one of those curtains all the time you were talking to the man who has just gone. I heard every word that was said. I know that he came to get from you a key which you found under the mattress of your late mistress' bed. I also know whom you meant when you spoke of 'he.' And I know more than that. I know how your mistress was killed—murdered, my girl—do you understand? That is why I came here to-day, disguised as one of the undertaker's men. I suspected you, and I know that you have been helping the man who killed your mistress. Do you know what that means? Do you know what it means to be an accessory to murder?"

"Oh, I am innocent—I am innocent. He —he told me it was something else. He said it was only to ask her for money. He—"

"Never mind that now. Listen to me. Do you want to be saved? Or do you want to go to prison, perhaps for several years?"

She only sobbed.

"I know who killed your mistress and I know the man who came here to-day," went on Blake. "The police are on their track and they will be arrested soon. Do you want to be arrested with them?"

"Oh! no, no, no."

"Then you must do as I tell you. If you obey me, I shall save you—if you do not I shall let you go to prison. Now what will you do?"

"I—I will do as you say. I am innocent —I didn't know—I was paid."

"Stop. You can talk of that later. Now I have some questions to ask you and I want you to answer each one truthfully and fully. If you don't, I shall know you are lying."

Then Blake began and put question after question to the trembling girl, speaking slowly, so that she should understand the weight and meaning of each word.

He forced her to reply in detail, and, when he had finished, he knew that he had at last succeeded in splitting asunder one of the thickest of the veils of mystery which had been spread in front of the case. Then he switched the subject.

"That man gave you a piece of paper with an address written on it," he said curtly. "Where is it?"

"Inside my dress."

"Let me see it."

The girl thrust a hand inside the front of her dress and, after fumbling about, brought out a small piece of folded paper. Blake opened it, and read what was written on it.

He was not surprised to find that it was the address of the same house in Church Street, Chelsea, to which Tinker had followed Jules on his arrival at Victoria. He handed the paper back.

"You will keep that appointment as you were ordered," he said. "To-night you will ask permission to go for a walk, as he told you. You will then follow his other instructions to the letter, reaching the door of this house at exactly ten o'clock. You'll then ring the bell and from that on you have nothing else to do. Do you understand?"

"Yes. sir. But what—what after that?"

"Nothing at all. That will be the end as far as you are concerned. And see that you do not fail or that you do not try to betray me. Those men will be in the hands of the police this night. If you betray me you will be with them. If you do as I order, I shall help you."

"I—I shall do as you say, sir."

"Very well. And say nothing of this to Mr. McMinn or the police. Now I shall go, and at ten o'clock I shall expect you to be at the door of that house in Chelsea."

With that Blake again fixed on his false beard and moustache, and a few minutes later, took his departure. He walked up to the Manor House Corner and there caught a tram down the Seven Sisters Road. He jumped off near the undertaker's and found that obliging gentleman in his private office.

Blake got out of his sombre clothes and into his own. Then, thanking the undertaker warmly for his help, he backed out the Grey Panther and started off at a fast pace for Baker Street.

"It's as clear as a pikestaff now," he muttered, as he mulled over the events of the past hour or so. "It is one of the strangest affairs that

I have ever come across. Who could have believed it? Who, even now, would believe it without absolutely irrefutable proof? Inspector Thomas will take some convincing, but, if he acts swiftly, then to-night—to-night he should net the birds who escaped him early this morning. And among them should be the man who murdered Mrs. McMinn."

12.   Tinker in Charge at Baker Street—The Warning Light—An Emissary of Willie Chang.

WHEN Blake, had departed for Finsbury Park, Tinker settled down to routine work. He had a good many entries to make in the "Index," and that alone promised to keep him busy most of the afternoon.

He ran up first to pay a brief visit to "Slick" Beecher, but found the wounded man asleep, so did not wake him. Then he returned to the consulting-room and sat down at his desk.

Now, as Tinker's desk was placed he was situated, when sitting at it, with his back to the door which gave on to the corridor leading along to the laboratory, and was partially facing the other door which opened into the main hall. In the corner opposite him was Blake's big mahogany desk.

He had, too, a full view of one of the windows—that nearest Blake's desk; but the other window, and that portion of the room back of him, could not be seen unless he turned. However, this lack of complete vision had been provided for quite recently, as shall soon be seen.

The new arrangement had been carried out immediately after a nasty raid on the house—a raid in which both Blake and Tinker had been caught napping from behind, and on that occasion Blake had said that he would ensure that such a thing could not occur again.

Tinker was soon engrossed in his work, for he had a keen interest in the material that went into the "Index," and it was his special pride to make it as detailed and at the same time as concise as Blake could, wish.

It was a sort of "Who's Who" and "What and How" of the criminal work!— a marvellous encyclopedia of all the criminal cases stretching back for more than twenty years, and there was nothing quite like it to be found any place else in the world.

Not even Scotland Yard could produce such a reference library as that "Index" of Blake's, which now consisted of more than a dozen big, fat volumes.

At the end of an hour Tinker was just finishing the last entry, dealing with a recent forgery case which they had handled. He was in the very act of reaching out for a piece of blotting-paper, when suddenly, just under his gaze, he saw a tiny red glow appear.

Embedded in the top of the desk was a little electric-light bulb, and it was this that had shown red. Just a tiny spot of colour it was, but it was enough for Tinker.

He did not turn his head. In fact, he did not vary his intended action in the slightest, except to lift his eyes just a trifle so he could look into a small bit of "fish-eye" mirror which was set in the desk in such fashion that he could command a clear view of all that part of the room behind him.

(A "fish-eye" mirror or lens is shaped in convex fashion as is the eye of a fish or bird, or, indeed, as the human eye, and gives a much greater range of vision than a flat mirror. Such a mirror can be made to reflect a very large area in proportion to its size, and, in the case of a lens, one can study practically a whole room through a tiny fish-eye glass that is no larger than a sixpenny-piece.)

And in the little mirror Tinker saw a very curious thing.

He saw the door behind him open inwards very, very slowly. It scarcely seemed to move at first, but then he could make out the ever-widening crack, and the next thing he saw was a hand, and followed by a wrist and arm. In that hand was grasped a long-bladed knife, and, in the shadowy background, Tinker thought he could just make out a menacing countenance.

Still he did not move. His fingers still hovered above the square of blotting-paper, and he picked it up as if to lay it on the page of the "Index." But as his fingers touched the top of the desk he pressed hard at a certain point.

The result was startling. Just what was set into motion it would have been hard to guess, but, on the instant that Tinker pressed the spot on the desk, the door through which that lean, yellow knife-hand was protruding slammed in hard against the arm as if someone had kicked it with terrific force.

Then Tinker came out of his seat with a bound, and, jerking out his automatic, whirled to face the menace.

He was just in time to see the knife drop to the floor from nerveless fingers. He saw the hand waggling weakly up, and down, and the wrist being dragged back and back between the edge of the door and the jamb until, despite the fact that the skin was being torn away, the person outside the door had managed to get it back as far as the wrist. And there, despite every effort, it stuck.

Tinker eased his tense attitude and grinned.

"Pretty work," he said aloud. "I'll bet any odds you want, my unknown friend, that you won't get your hand out of that trap. The bird who invented that neat, little snare knew what he was doing all right. Four hundred pounds pressure is keeping that door closed on your arm, and I guess you won't be able to overcome that. If you stick there long enough it will paralyse your whole arm, but I think I'll just have a look at you and find out who is so shy that he must come in that way when he calls—and with a knife in his hand, too."

He walked across and picked up the knife. He examined it for a few moments before tossing it on the desk.

"Chinese or Eastern, anyway," he muttered. "And that isn't hard to guess. That arm is the arm of a Chink or I never saw one. This is getting quite interesting. It's the first time we have had a chance to try this new trap the guv'nor installed, but it certainly is the cat's cuffs."

He turned and walked to the other door. Opening this, he stepped out into the main hall and made his way round to the side corridor which led to the laboratory. As he came close to the door there he could see the figure of a man standing just outside it, and, as it was a little gloomy in that part, he switched on an electric light.

Then he grinned as he saw a Chinaman, dressed in European garb, still trying to drag himself free from the trap which Tinker had sprung.

"You may as well save your strength, you yellow hound," he jeered. "You won't get out of that box in a hurry. It's got some of your precious Chinese puzzle boxes beaten to a frazzle. No, no—don't be so shy. Keep your head turned round. I want to have a good look at you."

He accompanied the words by shooting out a hand and gripping the Celestial by one ear. He gave a hard yank, and the fellow's head came round as if he had been an automaton. Tinker studied him silently for a few seconds. Then:

"Who are you?" he asked curtly.

"Not understand," was the sulky reply.

"You understand well enough. But you would lie about it, anyway. I suppose you are one of Willie Chang's men. Just thought you'd come along this afternoon and stick a nice long knife in someone here, didn't you? Clever little lad, aren't you? And Willie Chang thought he was quite smart when he sent you, didn't he?

"I suppose Willie was even shyer than you—didn't like to come in until he had a written invitation. Nice little fellow is Willie, but he'll get a written invite all right."

His bantering tone changed, and his young eyes grew hard.

"Yes, you yellow dog," he snarled as he gripped the Chink with both hands and began jerking his head back and forth, "thought you'd pull off another kill, didn't you? Well, I was ready for you, and you'll get worse than this before we finish with you. Now then, answer my questions, or I'll give you worse than you are getting. Who sent you here? Was it Willie Chang?"

"Willie Chang not know I come—I just come," gasped the Celestial.

"You lie, you dog! Give me the truth of that, or I tell you I will drag your yellow head off your body. Was it Willie Chang?"

Tinker had increased his pressure until the pain was more than even a stoical Chink could stand. The fellow gave a gasp and tried to speak. Tinker eased his hold a little, and repeated:

"Was it Willie Chang?"

"Willie Chang—he—send," came the choking answer, and Tinker desisted.

"That's enough for now," he said. "We'll see what the guv'nor has to say when he comes back. In the meantime, my yellow pigeon, I'll tie you up so you can't get away."

He ran along to the laboratory where he got some lengths of strong cord, and returning with these, he first secured the Chinaman's ankles. Next he got a good safe hitch round his left arm, and holding that jammed well up between his shoulder blades, pressed a secret button in the wall which released the door.

He pushed that inwards with his knee and caught hold of the right arm of his prisoner. It was completely nerveless by now, and he had no difficulty in dragging it back and tying it to the other.

Then he forced his man along inch by inch, into the consulting-room, and, suddenly, kicked him in the bend of the knees. The Chink went down flat on his face, and leaving him there for a moment, Tinker got out a wad of loose silk dusting cloth. He jammed this between the Chinaman's teeth, after which he bound a wide piece of cloth over his mouth.

That done, he dragged the would-be assassin close to the wall, and walking to the door, began whistling for Pedro.

In a few moments there was a lumbering rush down the front stairs as the big bloodhound came, almost bowling Tinker over as he

86

sprang through the doorway. Tinker wrestled with him for a few seconds, then he pointed towards the supine figure on the floor.

"Watch him, old fellow," he ordered.

Pedro walked gravely across and inspected the Chink. As the odour of the yellow man filled his nostrils he turned his head aside in distaste, for Pedro could not abide either yellow men or black.

But an order was an order, and he sat rigidly on guard ready with those great jaws at the slightest sign of movement.

Tinker grinned again and returned to the desk.

"And that's that," he remarked to Pedro as he sat down. "The guv'nor isn't having all the fun this afternoon, and I fancy he will be a little surprised when he sees what I have bagged in his absence."

He tackled the "Index" again, and was still working at it when Mrs. Bardell came in with his tea. The good soul did not see the bound celestial until she was well into the room, and then, as her eyes fell on him, she gave a startled squawk.

Her eyes bulged, and the tray canted at an angle of nearly thirty degrees. The cups and saucers and tea-pot began to slide and Tinker was just in time to grab the tray before disaster occurred.

"Such a house I never did see," panted the good soul as she relinquished the tray.

"I never could abide them yeller furriners. Why are you keeping him here, Master Tinker?"

"That's all right, Mrs. Bardell," returned Tinker, with a grin. "Didn't you hear the guv'nor say at breakfast this morning that he would have preferred scrambled eggs to poached?"

"But eggs—what has that to do with this furriner?"

"That's the guv'nor's scrambled egg," answered Tinker gravely, as he turned back to the tray. The housekeeper shook her head and went out muttering, and Tinker set to on the tea.

He had just finished when he heard a car outside and shortly after, a step in the hall. Then the door flew open and Blake strode in. His eyes fell at once on the bound and gagged Chinaman, and he turned to the lad with an inquiring look.

"The first bird in our new trap, guv'nor," said Tinker, reading the look. "I caught him not half an hour ago. He was paying us a visit, and this was his visiting card."

As he spoke he picked up the knife and held it out. Blake examined it briefly and tossed it on his desk.

"What else?" he asked curtly, walking over to the man and putting Pedro aside.

"He came from Willie Chang."

"Are you sure?"

"Well, sir, he denied it at first, but I tried one of their own little tricks on him and he changed his mind. I didn't press him for information after that."

Blake studied the fellow for a few moments; then he nodded his head.

"He told the truth there, Tinker. I remember now seeing him at the house in Limehouse last night. Tell me just what happened."

So Tinker told how he had been working at his desk when he had seen the little warning red bulb glow, and how, when he had pressed the secret switch, the door had jammed in, catching the prisoner by the arm just as the inventor of the system had planned it should. When he had finished Blake nodded in satisfaction.

"Good work, my lad. I fancy we shall find we made a good investment when we installed that trap. Without it, it is entirely possible that I should have returned to find you with a knife between your ribs."

"Well, guv'nor, I don't think you are far wrong. I didn't hear a sound—didn't suspect a thing until the little red bulb glowed. He came by the laboratory window. I saw it was open when I went along to get some cord. What will we do with him?"

"Put him in the laboratory for now. I'll telephone Inspector Thomas to send someone along to take him in charge. I want to talk to the inspector anyway. Tell Mrs. Bardell to bring me some tea, my lad, and then I want you to go into some of the back volumes of the 'Index' and find everything relating to the arrest of Willie Chang and his brother a few years ago. If my memory serves me I think you will find something there about some of the dope on the Changs being supplied to Scotland Yard by an anonymous letter writer, who, it was suspected, was a woman."

"Something developed this afternoon, guv'nor?" asked Tinker, with interest.

"A good deal. To-night, if all goes well, we shall see the finish of things, that is, if I can persuade Inspector Thomas to do as I wish. If he doesn't the birds have a good chance of escaping, and if they slip out of the net this time, we shall have slim hopes of catching them.

Now get that tea. I want to get the inspector here as quickly as possible."

13.   Blake Convinces inspector Thomas—Planning a Raid.

BUT I don't follow you, Blake."

"And I cannot be more explicit, inspector—not now, at any rate. If I were in a position to tell you more I should certainly do so. But I cannot tell you what I don't know."

Blake tossed his cigarette aside and reached for his pipe. Inspector Thomas absent-mindedly helped himself to one of Blake's Coronas and lit up before speaking again.

"Well," he said, at length, "you know that what you say is good enough for me. But you know, too, how things are at the Yard. That raid last night was such a fiasco that I am not keen on running another until I know where I am going to land."

Blake shrugged.

"Just as you please. I have told you that I can put you in the way to lay your hands on the man who murdered Mrs. McMinn. To do that I must have two warrants. I don't know myself the exact identity of the murderer, but I know where he can be found to-night. And I am dead certain that we can get him if we move swiftly."

"Can't you tell me more?" almost pleaded the inspector. "That business last night—"

"Oh, forget that," cut in Blake. "That was no fault of yours. You know what Willie Chang is as well as I. I was afraid you would be too late. It was the canal at the back that was the weak spot."

"I could have a conference to-night, and perhaps to-morrow we could carry out this other raid."

"Nothing doing. By to-morrow that yellow wave will have receded again to the East End. By to-morrow night it will have split into a hundred different currents. You will never get your men."

"Men? How many are there?"

"There are two as I said. One is a murderer, and—some other things. The other is guilty of two crimes that I know of, and I am beginning to suspect, of a third and fourth as well. I tell you, Thomas, I am giving you the chance to pull off one of the biggest coups of your career. I have never let you down yet, and I wouldn't waste time trying to persuade you now only this is, firstly and lastly, a case for the Yard to handle. If you don't want to take it up, then there is no more to be said. But I warn you that you will be letting a murderer slip through your hands."

"If you are sure—"

"Sure! Hang it, man, if you do as I say, I can promise you that before this night is over I will reveal things to you that you would not believe if I told them to you now. When I tell you it is one of the strangest cases that has ever come my way, perhaps you will understand, what I mean. This coup will be the biggest feather in your cap imaginable. But you've got to have courage and vision and—trust in me."

"Blake, you have never let me down yet, and I know you never will. The boys at the Yard have been ragging me about last night's fiasco, and I am a bit nervy today. But I'll do it. I place myself in your hands and I won't ask another question until the job is over."

"Good egg! I knew you'd come in." Blake turned to Tinker who was grinning across at him for the lad had been highly amused at the argument which had been going on between Blake and the inspector.

He knew that Blake would get his way in the long run. It had only been a question of time, to Tinker's mind, how long the inspector would hold out. And when Blake had said that it would he the biggest coup of his whole career Tinker knew it was all up.

But Blake did not smile although his eyes twinkled for just a moment.

"Get out the map book, Tinker, and turn up a detailed plan of Chelsea," he ordered. Then he rose:

"Come along, inspector. I have something in the laboratory to show you. We shall call it Exhibit 'A.' It is something Tinker bagged this afternoon while you were at the funeral."

Inspector Thomas rose obediently and followed Blake along to the laboratory. On the floor there lay the Chinaman whom Tinker had captured. Blake pointed to him.

"That is the only fish out of the pool you raided last night," he remarked. "He is small cheese compared to the men we shall try to bag to-night. But he is a cog in the machine. The definite charge against him will be one of trying to murder Tinker. That is the prisoner I said I had for you. We shall turn him over to your men when they arrive."

"How did Tinker catch him?" asked Thomas, with interest.

"I shall show you—in confidence," responded Blake. "Come along."

They walked back along the corridor, but outside the door leading into the consulting-room Blake made the inspector pause.

"Stand just here," he ordered. "That's it. Now I shall close the door almost. Put your arm through as if you were holding a weapon of some sort in your hand. That's it. Now you will imagine that Tinker is to be your victim. You have sneaked along here and found him engrossed in his work. Now watch."

With that, Blake shot out a quick word to Tinker, who was seated at his desk. The lad jammed his finger down on the secret button, and on the same instant the door closed with no little force on the inspector's arm, causing him to give a startled yelp. Blake smiled as he touched the release button in the wall and pushed the door open.

"That is how Tinker did it," he said, as he entered the consulting-room. "Look here on his desk. See that little light? Well, whenever the door over there is opened it causes this little red bulb to light up. That is a warning, and if you look in this fish-eye mirror you will see that one can survey almost the whole of the room behind one. What then? Simply press this little secret spring here and hey presto! Bang goes the door, catching in the trap whatever is there. I have the same arrangement on my desk. Rather neat, isn't it?"

"Well, I'm blessed," exclaimed the inspector. "You folks here are certainly up to date. We haven't anything like that at the Yard."

"Nor do you need them. You are too well protected," responded Blake dryly. "Now come here and study this plan of Chelsea."

They pored over the plan for some time, Blake marking off Church Street, and then putting a little blue cross where No. 182A stood. Even on the plan it was possible to see that the place was of some considerable area, and from the information he had received from Jimmy, the newspaper seller, Blake knew that it was entirely surrounded by a high wall.

"You see, it is quite isolated in a way," he said. "It fronts on Church Street, as you see. This wall here and this one here divided it off completely from the properties adjoining on either side. At the back you find, here, a narrow lane. There is, according to my informant, a big gate there so we shall have to bear that in mind. It is the front and the back, and if you are ready I shall tell you what I think is our best plan. I shall also tell you why I choose ten o'clock to-night as the hour for striking."

"Proceed," returned the inspector laconically.

"We shall want the same number of men you used last night—forty. We may not need half that number, but we can't afford to take any chances. I want to make a clean sweep. Also I want you to arrange for two heavy motor lorries to be close at hand shortly before ten o'clock."

"Why the motor lorries? I can understand about the men, but not about them unless you want to pile the prisoners into them"

"That is one purpose for which they can be used, but not the primary one. I want them to drive along just before we strike and take up a position at the back—one to be drawn right across the lane at this end and the other across the other end."

"Ah! I get you now. You want to block the alley."

"Exactly."

"You think they will try to make a getaway by that?"

"They will try every hole. We don't want to leave one unguarded. We must bag the whole lot to-night. Remember what I said, Thomas, I shall give you the person who murdered Mrs. McMinn if you do as I say. And I am willing to bet that so far neither you nor the local inspector at Finsbury Park has the slightest vestige of a clue."

"I'll be honest and say we haven't. And I'm hanged if I know how you have fallen on to one. But I said I wouldn't ask any more questions, and I won't. I'll arrange about the lorries as you suggest."

"Then that is all for now. Just off Oakley Street, which runs off the King's Road in Chelsea, there is a short street known as Phene Street which connects Oakley Street with Oakley Crescent. In that little backwater is a quiet public house known as the Phene Arms. I know the people who own it. They are to be trusted entirely. In the back is a small but very secluded little saloon bar. Meet me there at half-past nine this evening, and I shall tell you the next step. By that time all your men should be in a position to close in at the signal."

"I know the Phene Arms all right. I'll be there. But I think you might tell me what the signal will be."

"So I shall. At a few minutes before ten a woman should get off a number eleven 'bus at the corner of the King's Road and Church Street. She should then walk up Church Street, and, at precisely ten o'clock, she should ring the bell at the door of number 182A. The moment she does that, inspector, you will have the signal. There is always the chance that she will not turn up, but I am gambling on that. If she fails us then we shall have to attack in any case. But that signal is ours, because it is also a signal which the enemy will understand."

And with that cryptic remark Blake rose.

14. The Raid at Chelsea—Brief But Desperate Escape and Disaster.

AT precisely half-past nine that evening Sexton Blake entered the Phene Arms, the quiet little inn of which he had spoken to the inspector. The first person he saw was Thomas, standing at the bar talking with the proprietor, Mr. Lukey, while the latter's cheery and popular son, John, hovered close at hand.

As Blake entered he was greeted with a genial "Good-evening," but his name was not mentioned, for there were three or four other customers in the bar at the time.

Apparently the inspector had been doing some spade work before Blake's arrival, for Blake saw a quick sign pass between the proprietor and the man from Scotland Yard, after which the latter shot a meaning look at Blake.

The inspector then walked out, turning as if to go towards the back of the premises, and, after leisurely drinking a glass of beer, Blake followed.

As he turned the corner of a short corridor he found John standing waiting for him.

"In here, Mr. Blake," he whispered. "You and the inspector can use the parlour."

Blake nodded his thanks, and opened a door opposite him, where he found the inspector ensconced in an easy-chair. Two glasses of beer were waiting for them, and as Blake sat down Thomas said:

"Well, everything is ready on my part of the job. I have thirty-five men posted, and, at ten minutes to ten, they will begin to close in. The lorries are standing by in the King's Road. They will pull into position at the same time."

"Splendid. I had a word with an agent of mine on my way here. His report is that there are people at the house which is our objective, so I am hoping our birds have not cleared out. We might walk along soon and take up position near the corner of the street. I am anxious to be there when the young woman of whom I spoke should get off the bus."

"All right."

They finished their drinks and rose. Passing through the corridor they emerged into Phene Street, and then walked up Margaretta Terrace, which runs parallel to Oakley Street, until they came into the latter thoroughfare, just a short distance from King's Road.

They strolled leisurely up King's Road until they came to a couple of big, covered motor-lorries standing by the kerb, and Blake knew, when the inspector touched him on the arm, that these were the two police vehicles.

In fact, just as they were passing them the one in front started off, and a moment later the second lumbered after it.

Across King's Road a sharp eye might have seen a man here and a man there moving along in the direction of Church Street; but no casual pedestrian would have noticed any concerted plan in it, all so quietly was it effected.

They kept on until they had almost reached the corner of Church Street, and there Blake led the way across the road.

They took up a position just a few yards from the corner, and stood smoking in the shadow while the hands of a nearby clock crept slowly round to the hour of ten.

Blake was watching every bus which came along, the traffic at that hour of the night being much lighter than earlier in the day. More than one No. 11 rumbled by, and several stopped at the corner of Church Street. But, although he watched keenly, he could see no signs of Maggie Williams.

The hands of the big clock opposite were just touching on the hour when another No. 11 appeared, and drew up at the corner of the street.

Blake leant forward to see who got out, and, as he saw a young woman descend and pass directly under the light, he gave a little sigh of relief.

"She cut it fine, but she has made it," he whispered. "Come on—we must follow her."

Inspector Thomas had been following the line of Blake's gaze, and now he gave vent to a low exclamation.

"That girl," he muttered, "I have seen her before. Her face is quite familiar to me. Why—where—why, hang it all, Blake, she is the servant girl at the villa in Woodberry Down."

"Quite so," responded Blake. "She is also our signal. Hurry up, or we shall miss the whole show."

They strode along Church Street, keeping some little distance behind the girl. From time to time they caught sight of a man here, and another there, sometimes twos and threes, and all standing in the shadow as if idly talking.

They gave no sign, but a score of pairs of eyes was on them, watching their every move, for they had been recognised the moment they entered the street.

Some little distance along Maggie Williams paused, as if uncertain of the house for which she was looking. They could see her bend forward to study a number, then she suddenly disappeared, and Blake quickened his pace.

"Hurry!" he whispered. "She's going up the path now. Let her get right on to the porch and ring. They may be on the look-out for her. But the moment she touches the bell, give it about three seconds, and then let that whistle of yours go rip as hard as you can."

They were at the gate by now, and, crouching back in the shadow, they could see the silhouette of the girl on the porch. She seemed to hesitate at first, but then she lifted her arm, and they saw her hand go out. Blake counted three, and then he jerked his head round.

"Split that whistle—hard!" he snapped. "Then come on."

He was clawing out his automatic when the night was shattered by the sound of the blast which the inspector blew. Three times he sent it shrilling out, and then, as figures began running towards him from a dozen different points, he raced up the path after Blake.

Blake was trying to reach the porch before the door should be closed. He had seen it just begin to open when he told the inspector to blow his whistle, and he could see Maggie Williams cowering back in terror in one corner.

He had one foot on the top step when someone inside started to slam the door hard. Blake took the porch in one leap and hurled his full weight against the portal. It flew back, sending the person inside sprawling. He lurched in, almost losing his balance, recovered, and then stood gazing along a wide, almost bare hall which seemed utterly devoid of any signs of human beings.

He looked down and saw a smallish man trying to scramble to his feet. The fellow had the cut of a Latin about him, and Blake knew he must be simply an unimportant underling.

He grabbed him by the scruff of the neck and flung him out across the porch, almost bowling the inspector over. One of the police caught the man, and then Blake raced on, making for the bottom of the stairs on the right-hand side of the hall.

The inspector was close after him, followed by a score of men, and just then the whole place inside seemed to spring to life. At the top of the stairs two figures appeared, and a hail of bullets came pelting down as two automatics spat viciously.

Blake saw that one of the figures was Willie Chang, but he did not know the other man. So far, Jules, the Frenchman, was not to be seen.

Just then two doors at the side of the hall flew open, and a motley crowd poured through—every man-jack armed either with revolver or knife.

The police divided as if by prearranged signal, while Blake, the inspector, and half a dozen others tore up the stairs, full in the face of the deadly hail of lead which was pouring about and over them.

How they went through that rain of death no one can tell. But go through they did, and Blake was almost at the top when Willie Chang pulled his trigger down on a dead pistol. He hurled the heavy weapon full at Blake, and turned to run.

The other man hesitated, then he followed suit, and the human flood poured over the top of the stairs and along a hall which seemed to lead towards the rear.

Willie Chang jerked open a door on the left and disappeared. His companion was hot after him, and Blake was less than two yards behind. The second man slammed the door in Blake's face, but, before he could lock it, Blake had dashed it open, and was just in time to see the silhouette of a figure on the window-sill. Then it flashed from view; but a second later a second figure went over the sill.

As it disappeared Blake flung himself forward and looked out. It was not much of a drop to the ground, and he figured if Willie Chang could make it he could. He flung a leg over, slid down and hung for a moment by his hands. Then he let go, keeping his joints loose as he did so.

He landed with scarcely a shock, and, jumping up, saw the two fugitives racing across the lawn towards a long, low building which seemed to have been built in one corner of the grounds.

Inspector Thomas was a heavy man and not young; but he was game to the core, and, as he looked back, Blake saw him lumbering along after him. Behind him came a string of his men, and with a shout Blake dashed on.

Just then he heard shots and cries at the back of the house, and he knew the police in the lane must be attacking from that point. He gave another loud cry to attract their attention if possible, then he reached the low building in the corner.

He hurled himself against a door. It burst open, and he stumbled in just in time to see Willie Chang and the other man take a flying leap on to the footboard of a big, red-painted racing car that was even then beginning to move.

By the single light which burned in the garage Blake could recognise Jules, the Frenchman, at the wheel. He drew up and took a pot-shot at him, but must have missed, for the car went out through open double swing-doors with a jerk, and then, swinging almost on two wheels, disappeared from view.

Blake tore after, followed by the others. He reached the lane at the back, realising now that the garage had been built in that corner for just such a purpose as it had served that night—in order that quick getaway might be made in case of a raid.

He reached the lane in time to hear the car roaring along with the cut-out wide open. He saw something lurching from side to side, then he heard the sudden scream of brakes, followed by a terrific impact, a wild rattling sound that lasted several seconds, and then the upper end of the lane was suddenly illuminated as a great burst of flame shot up.

By that torch they could see what had happened. The Frenchman had spotted the lorry drawn across the upper end too late to draw up. He must have been travelling at the rate of a good fifty miles an hour when he hit it.

The heavy racer had cut almost clean through the big lorry, and the two vehicles were in a wild tangle of wreckage.

One petrol-tank had burst and caught fire, and even as they gazed, shocked and spellbound at the wreckage, they saw another great flame shoot up, telling them that the second tank had burst as well.

They raced along, followed by a score or more of police. Already some of the inspector's men were trying to drag the four men out of the terrible furnace into which they had plunged.

Two unconscious figures lay at one side, but it was quite hopeless to try and reach the others. No human being could approach within a dozen feet of that blazing furnace. All they could do was to stand back, appalled, while the flames did their work.

And it was not until the ghastly holocaust was almost over that Sexton Blake found Tinker standing by his side and heard the lad say:

"Chang and one of the others were in there, guv'nor. The Frenchman is just conscious, and wants to say something. I asked him if he would say it to Sexton Blake, and he begged me to bring you to him. The other man is already gone, and Jules can't last long."

"I'll come at once."

With that Blake turned and hurried across to where Jules lay.

15. Blake Sums Up—Conclusion.

SEXTON BLAKE had not exaggerated when he told Inspector Thomas that, if the raid that night were successful, it would be the biggest coup in his— the inspector's—whole career. It proved to be just that, for, at that house of evil in Church Street, they came upon more even than Blake had expected to find.

He had suspected the existence of it, but he had had nothing more definite to go on than the few scattered words which Jimmie, the little street rat, had whispered in his ear that evening in the consulting-room at Baker Street,

The whole thing was, as Blake had acknowledged, one of the strangest cases that he had ever tackled, and one of the most complicated as well. It was a maze of wheels within wheels; it was a tangled scheme which had had its genesis away back twenty years and more before.

It needed Blake to elucidate each point that went to make up the fabric of the case, and there could be no better exposition of how that well-trained mind had applied itself to the problem than that which he gave to Inspector Thomas and Tinker in the consulting-room some time after midnight that night, when he was seated at his desk, his clean-cut face as expressionless as a mask.

In one of the low saddle-bag chairs the inspector reclined, one of Blake's Coronas between his teeth and a stiff whisky-and-soda at his elbow; in another of the saddlebags was Tinker, curled up like a cat, his young face alight with admiration—and more than that—as he drank in every word that Blake was saying.

Blake had been dealing with the actual facts of the raid when he paused to pour himself a drink and light his pipe. Then he sank back and proceeded:

"From the very first the case began to open up with a rapidity which was almost bewildering. I'll try to give you the points just as I struck them, inspector, and when you have heard all you will understand why I could not tell you more than I did.

"I shall begin at the moment when I drove down to Woodberry Down with you on the Sunday evening. It was not difficult to size up things in the sitting-room. It was obvious from the first that the woman had been killed by a shot fired by someone standing just inside the door of the room. The direction of flight of the bullet was beyond doubt.

"I at once thought that, at that hour of the evening, with people in the street such a short distance away and other people living near at hand, that the sound of a shot should have been heard. I did not think of an air-pistol then, but the moment I saw the bullet which had been extracted at the post-mortem I thought it very probable that an air-pistol had been used.

"The bullet was of foreign manufacture— Italian, as I can prove by showing you one of the examples in my own collection. And I knew that such a bullet was very often used in a very powerful type of Italian pistol which is discharged by compressed air. From that it wasn't very far to go to find an explanation as to why the sound had not been heard. Very well.

"I went on the theory that John McMinn was innocent. That was sheer instinct. The man was transparently honest, and it was not difficult to eliminate him. Then who remained? Only the servant— Maggie Williams. While you spoke to her in the dining-room I watched her carefully, and I did not like the look of fear which was in her eyes. I did not think she had done the job. Her alibi was too good for that, but I thought she might know more than she said. By her type—she is a good-looking girl, but not over-intelligent—I thought she might be under the influence of someone else. So I determined to keep an eye on her.

"In the meantime I was given an opportunity by McMinn to examine the different rooms. I spent some time in his wife's apartment, and while poking about there I found something that caused me to think furiously. You remember the blonde wig to which you called my attention?"

"Of course."

"Well, in a drawer in the cupboard in her room, I found more wigs, and they were both blonde and coal black. Now, I asked myself, why did Mrs. McMinn wear a black wig as well as a blonde. I asked her husband casually if she ever wore a black wig, and he at once said that he had never seen such a thing. Then, I persisted in asking myself, why did she have them?

"I examined them closely, for, in the lining of the blonde wig which she was wearing at the time of her death, I had seen a little green silk cross which told me quite a lot. I found that same green silk cross in the lining of all the other wigs, and, if my memory served me rightly, I knew that silk cross to be the private mark of one of the most exclusive and expensive hair dressers in Europe—one Jules, of the Champs Elysees, in Paris.

"My next move was to go across to Paris. I need not dwell on that in detail, but I found out more there than I had hoped. I discovered that Jules had a customer in England, who was known on their books simply as Madame Berthe. Now Mrs. McMinn's Christian name was Bertha, and Berthe is the French rendering of that name. That seemed more than just coincidence to me. I discovered, further, that while these wigs had been made by Jules— at the rate of two each year or so—no charge appeared on the books, and, in addition, they were invariably taken to England by a special messenger, who travelled to Paris for that express purpose.

"What was the explanation of such an extraordinary thing? In what way could this queer business be connected with the fat, middle-aged, placid wife of a foreman printer living in a London suburb? It seemed utterly beyond reason. One could understand a very wealthy Society woman, who wished to keep her little secret to herself, sending a messenger across to Paris to bring her wigs back, but not the wife of a man like John McMinn. And why the two colours? That, I confess, puzzled me more than anything else. Or, I should say, that and the fact that there was no record that Jules charged this particular client anything for the wigs. And each one could not have been valued at less than ten thousand francs.

"I began to feel then that there was something very—very obscure which must be got at. I had had the whole life history of the dead woman from her husband. It was simple and, on the face of it, as wide open as the day. In the whole course of it there was only one period which wasn't perfectly ordinary. That period was one year which she spent in Paris, more than twenty years ago. I thought then, and I know now, that it was this year which must answer the riddle. So I set myself to discover what could have happened in that year which would explain a murder twenty and more years later.

"Well, I know to-night. I have not learned the truth as I had expected. But I know it from the dying confession which Jules made to me. And this it is.

"The woman, who was known as Mrs. McMinn, was one of the strangest beings who ever lived. It is impossible to find a better description for her than to say that she was a female Jekyll and Hyde. She was, in one phase of her life, a perfectly normal, quiet-living woman; a good housewife, a devout churchgoer, and respected and looked up to by all who knew her. In the other phase she was a devil incarnate; a foul fiend who has spread ruin in a hundred ways; a harpy who battened on the innocent and helpless; a trader in human bodies; a peddler in deadly drugs; an ogress who devoured all that came her way. It is the most appalling experience of her sex that I have ever struck."

Blake paused, and the inspector shifted his position.

"I—I can scarcely credit what you say, Blake. But, of course, I know now it is true."

"That is exactly why I would not tell you all I knew before. I knew you would think I had suddenly gone mad. And I shouldn't have blamed you. It is almost inconceivable, but it is true. In that house of evil to-night we tracked down others of the gang. The two who matter are dead— dead by their own act. The others are safely under lock and key. In that hour, what did you find?

"You found an amazing stock of drugs of all descriptions. You found the complete paraphernalia for gambling in every known way. And, above all, you found evidence that the woman was the prime mover in other ghastly businesses. Isn't that proof?

"Who was the head and tail of the whole affair? The woman known as Madame Bertha. Who supplied cocaine and morphia and opium and heroin to half the dope peddlers of London? Madame Bertha. Who had agents in every quarter of the metropolis, seeking fools to inveigle to the gaming tables, and from that to drugs? Madame Bertha.

"And who was this Madame Bertha? Mrs. John McMinn, wife of a foreman printer in a London suburb who, as far as was known, seldom, if ever, left her home. Then how did she do it? How was it possible?

"Even yet it seems incredible. Listen! This woman—this good woman in one case, and this foulest of foul fiends in another, went to Paris as a young girl. While she was there, she fell under the influence of the man known as Jules. At the time he was a young apprentice to his trade—an apprentice in the day-time, but a frequenter of apache resorts at night. The girl met him, and it needed just that touch to cause to spring to life and flower the hidden cancer which some terrible freak of nature had sown inside her soul. She plunged into the utmost depths of the lowest life of Paris. We can imagine the torture her other self must have undergone when it was uppermost. But she was the creature of this inner devil while it was awake, and she touched the bottom-most nit of all that the city of evil could show her.

"I suspected this; it was the only thing to explain what seemed impossible to explain; and Jules, to-night, before he died, told me the truth. How she broke away from it and returned to England, we don't know and never shall. But she did return, and we can imagine her better self urging her to marry simple John McMinn so that she should have a sheet anchor.

"Now look how Fate, if one can call it that, played its devilish prank upon her. If John McMinn had worked the normal hours which other men work, all might have gone well, and that hydra-headed monster might have been strangled. But that was not to be. His duties took him from home at an early hour of the evening, and kept him away until the day came. What happened during the hours of night—during the hours when all the forces of evil are abroad? The monster arose and took the woman into its power. The old cancer broke out afresh, and, before long, she was leaving her home as soon as the hours of darkness made it safe.

"She proceeded with all the cunning which the foul thing inside her could inspire. Slowly but surely she got in deeper and deeper. She began just by communicating again with her Paris lover. He would come across to London, and the two would indulge in nameless orgies. But the hydra-headed monster was not to be content with that for long. He demanded more and more, and still more; and as the years passed the business of Madame Bertha was built up.

"She became the real fountain-head of the drug and other traffic in London. She amassed a fortune—that fat, placid wife of a foreman printer who dozed away her days in a quiet London suburb. It was some time before the arrest of Willie Chang, over that old affair, that the Chinaman became part of her machine. Then she thought he double-crossed her, and she betrayed him. I have been re-reading the notes I have of that case, and, if you will do the same, you will recall that most of the information about Willie Chang and his brother came by anonymous letters, which it was suspected a woman wrote. Well, it was Madame Bertha who wrote those letters. And Willie Chang got to know it.

"When he came out of prison he was deported, but he managed to slip back into England, and he set about planning his revenge. He ferreted out her secret, and when he had done that he had a strong card. Then he got in touch with Jules, and because the Frenchman was getting tired of his middle-aged agent, because she was growing mean, and Willie Chang told him there were thousands of pounds to divide, he joined forces with the Chinaman.

"Together the pair planned to get rid of her. They studied the situation carefully, and fixed on the servant girl at the villa as a necessary accomplice. Chang got in touch with her through one of his tools who made love to her. It was not hard then to overcome her scruples. She had no idea that murder was contemplated; but she was willing to listen to her lover and believe the stories he told her, because she had discovered that her mistress left the house secretly three or four nights a week.

"That was not difficult. You remember the stretch of garden at the back that runs to the bank of the river?"

"Yes."

"She went that way. She would then pass along the bank behind the hedge to the bridge, where a closed car was waiting. On those occasions she was Madame Berthe, and Madame Berthe it was who wore the black wigs. From there she would drive to the house in Church Street, and there, during the hours of the night, she would ply her vile trade. But she was always away at a good hour, like some infernal Cinderella, and, when John McMinn returned home, he invariably found his wife in bed and, apparently, asleep.

"That is nearly all. As soon as Willie Chang had found out all he needed to know he forced the girl, Maggie Williams, to secrete him in the house. Owing to the fact that McMinn had hurt his arm at work, he was forced to remain at home for a few days. It was impossible then for the woman to leave, and Chang knew this through the servant. He also knew the routine of the household, and on the Saturday night he forced the servant to conceal him in one of the upstairs attics, where he would be perfectly safe.

"All he had to do then was to watch for a chance. He was lurking about the house all day Sunday, and in the evening when John McMinn went out to post a letter, his opportunity came. We shall never know if he spoke to the woman before shooting. We shall never know if she was conscious of the identity of her assassin. But we do know that it was Willie Chang who killed her, and that he, the murderer, is now facing a higher tribunal than any earthly court.

"I was at the house when you and Inspector Brown followed the funeral cortège. I was there disguised as one of the undertaker's men, and I managed by a little finesse to make the girl think I had gone. In reality I was concealed behind a curtain in the sitting-room, and I was standing in that spot when Jules arrived on the scene.

"He had come in place of Chang to secure a certain key which the girl had been ordered to find. She had done so, and gave it to him. I could hear every word that was said, and I could tell that the girl was in a state of terror. I did not interfere, for I knew I should gain more by waiting. As soon as Jules was gone I tackled the girl. I revealed my identity and terrified her more than he had. Then I learned the truth.

"From what she said I figured the key he had come for must be the key of a safe, and now we know it was the key of the big safe at the house in Church Street. We know what wealth was stored there, and that Chang and Jules were going to divide the loot to-night before clearing out. Those thousands, built on evil, will never be accepted by John McMinn. But they can go to help those who have suffered through the vile fiend which slobbered over them. And that is but right and just.

"But to get back to the girl. She had told Chang that I was on the case. You already know how Tinker and I were discovered in Chang's joint in Limehouse. We managed to escape, and Chang decided that it was too dangerous to leave the girl at the villa any longer. He was afraid she would be forced to confess. So he sent a message by Jules that she was to come to the house in Church Street to-night, that he would guarantee her safety until the affair had blown over. She was not such a fool as not to be able to see that her flight would look bad, but she dared not refuse. Or she would not have done so if I had not terrified her, for her own good, more than had Jules. She did not dream that the moment she entered that house she would be swallowed up as completely as if she had stepped off into space; that she would simply have been shipped off to South America with those other poor girls who, thank Heaven, we were in time to rescue.

"I forced her to tell me all, and through her I got the links I needed. From that I was able to lay my plans, and—well, my dear fellow, that is all."

The inspector roused himself. So absorbed had he been in what Blake had been saying that he had forgotten his drink and allowed his cigar to die.

"All," he blurted explosively— "all? By the pink-toed prophet of Bloomsbury, Blake, it is the most extraordinary relation I have ever heard, and I am no chicken in the coop of crime. All? Man, I give it to you—there isn't another man living who could have laid that crime bare as you have done; who could have linked up those incidents of more than twenty years ago with this crime of to-day in a London suburb. And, believe me, I realise fully that it is, indeed, just as you say—the biggest coup I have ever pulled off. But it was entirely due to you."

"Hear, hear!" put in Tinker.

Blake rose a little wearily and reached for the decanter.

"Rot!" he said shortly. "Anyone could have done the same by applying the simple principles which govern the science of criminology and logic, making an allowance for the fact that there is always room for the seemingly impossible to happen. And that's enough of that for to-night. Say when, inspector."

THE END.

www.ingramcontent.com/pod-product-compliance
Lightning Source LLC
Chambersburg PA
CBHW031851170626
46807CB00004B/1670